# A TIME OF DAY

## Francis Durbridge

WILLIAMS AND WHITING

Cover design by Timo Schroeder

9781912582457

Williams & Whiting (Publishers)

15 Chestnut Grove, Hurstpierpoint,

West Sussex, BN6 9SS

Titles by Francis Durbridge published by Williams & Whiting

1   The Scarf (tv serial)
2   Paul Temple and the Curzon Case (radio serial)
3   La Boutique (radio serial)
4   The Broken Horseshoe (tv serial)
5   The Plays for Radio Vol 1
6   Send For Paul Temple (radio serial)

Murder At The Weekend – the rediscovered newspaper serials and short stories

Also published by Williams & Whiting:

Francis Durbridge : The Complete Guide
By Melvyn Barnes

Titles by Francis Durbridge to be published by Williams & Whiting:
A Case For Paul Temple
A Game of Murder
A Man Called Harry Brent
A Time of Day
Bat Out of Hell
Breakaway – The Family Affair
Breakaway – The Local Affair
Death Comes to the Hibiscus (stage play – writing as Nicholas Vane)
La Boutique
Melissa
Murder In The Media
My Friend Charles
Paul Temple and the Alex Affair
Paul Temple and the Canterbury Case (film script)

This book reproduces Francis Durbridge's original script together with the list of characters and actors of the BBC programme on the dates mentioned, but the eventual broadcast might have edited Durbridge's script in respect of scenes, dialogue and character names.

# INTRODUCTION

Perhaps at the outset I should put Francis Durbridge (1912-98) in context for those who might be unaware of the considerable extent of his career. Viewers who remember his television serials might not realise – unless they have heard twenty-first century repeats of his radio serials – that by the time he turned to television in the 1950s he had already been arguably the most popular writer of mystery thrillers for BBC radio since the 1930s. In 1938 he had found the niche in which he was to establish his name, when his radio serial *Send for Paul Temple* was so successful that it led to a series that continued for thirty years and created an enormous UK and European fanbase. So it was not surprising, while continuing to write for radio, that he turned to the newer medium of television – and in doing so, he presented in 1952 *The Broken Horseshoe* as the first thriller serial on British television.

*A Time of Day* was Francis Durbridge's seventh BBC television serial, transmitted in six thirty-minute episodes from 13 November to 18 December 1957. The producer/director, Alan Bromly, was to remain the guru for most of Durbridge's television serials, just as Martyn C. Webster had been for Durbridge's radio serials. The Durbridge/Bromly television partnership, dating from Durbridge's fourth serial *Portrait of Alison* in 1955, could always be relied upon to conjure up all the tried and tested Durbridge ingredients – numerous red herrings, a stunning cliff-hanger at the end of each episode, and the certainty that viewers should not believe anything that anyone says.

*A Time of Day*, one of his best, was no exception. As always it boasted a quality cast – with Stephen Murray suffering deliciously, just as he had done in *My Friend Charles* (1956) and was again to do in *The Scarf* (1959).

Sadly *A Time of Day* was never repeated, so it is reasonable to suppose that no recording has survived – and although it was soon adapted as a novel, there is now the first opportunity to read Durbridge's recently discovered original television script.

By that time Francis Durbridge was established as the foremost exponent of the thriller serial on UK television, the master of plots that twisted and turned while his protagonist struggled in a web spun by someone who remained a mystery until the final episode. Another feature of Durbridge thrillers was that they were refreshingly British, in a period when many television crime series were imported from the USA – a factor that also applied to Durbridge's nearest BBC television rival, Nigel Kneale, whose science fiction serials involving Professor Bernard Quatermass were also popular.

Durbridge's sophistication was certainly in stark contrast to American sock-in-the-jaw action. For many years since the 1930s, despite his Britishness or possibly because of it, his radio serials had been broadcast in various European countries, in their own languages and using their own actors. It was therefore not surprising that he also became a great attraction on European television screens, from the time when his sixth television serial (*The Other Man*, 1956) was adopted by German television in 1959. His seventh, *A Time of Day*, appeared on German television as *Es ist soweit* (21 October – 7 November 1960, six episodes), translated by Marianne de Barde and directed by Hans Quest; on Italian television as *Paura per Janet* (2 – 18 December 1963, six episodes), translated by Franca Cancogni and directed by Daniele D'Anza; and on Polish television as *W biały dzień* (11 – 25 November 1971, three episodes), translated by Kazimierz Piotrowski and directed by Jan Bratkowski.

After *A Time of Day*, every Durbridge television serial was seen in countries throughout Europe. They attracted an almost unbelievably large body of viewers, and today Durbridge's name might possibly remain better known abroad than in his home country. It is many years since he achieved iconic status when German commentators described his serials as *straßenfeger* (street sweepers), because a great swathe of the population stayed at home to listen to them on the radio or watch them on television.

At one time adaptations of Durbridge serials for the cinema were popular – and viewers of Talking Pictures TV still have the opportunity to see them today. From 1946 onwards, four film adaptations of his early Paul Temple radio serials were made and were followed by film versions of his first five BBC television serials *The Broken Horseshoe*, *Operation Diplomat*, *The Teckman Biography* (filmed as *The Teckman Mystery*), *Portrait of Alison* and *My Friend Charles* (filmed as *The Vicious Circle*). But sadly the cinema world appears to have lost interest in Durbridge after the mid-1950s – not enough sex and explosions, probably – whereas his radio and television careers and later his theatrical career proceeded apace.

*A Time of Day* was published as a novel (Hodder & Stoughton, December 1959). Then rather unusually, soon after its book publication it was serialised in the weekly magazine *Woman's Day* in eleven instalments (Vol 5 No. 91 to No. 101, 6 February – 16 April 1960). Magazine serialisations of novels were quite common at that time, but usually they were abridged versions of novels yet to be published, while the *Woman's Day* serialisation used almost the full book with minimal editing, supplemented with atmospheric illustrations by John Heseltine. The first instalment was headed: "For the first time in any woman's magazine – a tensely thrilling Francis Durbridge serial." European translations of the novel appeared in Germany as *Es ist soweit*, in Holland as *Er is een kind ontvoerd*, in Spain as

*Un momento del día*, in Norway as *Avgjørelsens øyeblikk* and in Poland as *W biały dzień*.

For those who like audiobooks, the English version of the novel appeared on six CDs read by Greg Wise (AudioGo, 2013). But in the absence of a television recording, let's now enjoy this welcome discovery of the original television script.

**Melvyn Barnes**
Author of Francis Durbridge: The Complete Guide (Williams & Whiting, 2018)

# A TIME OF DAY

A television serial in six episodes

## By FRANCIS DURBRIDGE

First broadcast on BBC Television
13<sup>th</sup> November – 18<sup>th</sup> December, 1957
Directed by Alan Bromly

### CAST:

| | |
|---|---|
| Clive Freeman | Stephen Murray |
| Lucy Freeman | Dorothy Alison |
| Anna | Marianne Walla |
| Janet Freeman | Angela Ramsden |
| Mrs. Denby | Iris Baker |
| Detective Inspector Kenton | Raymond Huntley |
| Sergeant Brooks | Edwin Brown |
| Sergeant Williams | Frank Pemberton |
| Laurence Hudson | John Sharplin |
| Ursula Wayne | Anna Barry |
| Detective Superintendent Wilde | Ernest Hare |
| Ruth Calthorpe | Annabel Maule |
| Barbara Barstow | Hazel Hughes |
| Roy Pelford | Gerald Cross |
| Lomax | Robert Hunter |
| Nelson | Maurice Durant |
| Fred Wade | Lane Meddick |
| Nurse Lynn | Anne Ridler |
| Robert Stevens | Richard Bebb |
| George Harris | Peter Halliday |
| Eddie | Freddie Watts |
| Sergeant Bailey | Edward Dentith |
| Sergeant Davis | Hedger Wallace |
| Jack Stafford | Frank Pettitt |

# EPISODE ONE

OPEN TO: Drawing Room at Amberley, a lovely house in Buckinghamshire, about twenty-five miles from London. *CLIVE FREEMAN is sitting at a writing bureau reading a letter, a pile of correspondence by his side. CLIVE is a distinguished, studious man in his thirties. The bureau stands in a corner of an attractive room. LUCY FREEMAN enters. She is a shade younger than her husband: good-looking with a strong personality. She is dressed for going out and her attitude towards CLIVE is tense and distinctly unfriendly. CLIVE turns as she enters, letters in hand.*

CLIVE: (*Surprised*) Are you going out?

LUCY: Yes.

CLIVE: You know I'm expecting Laurence.

LUCY: Laurence is your problem. I've got mother to contend with.

CLIVE: (*Rising*) Oh, have you spoken to her?

LUCY: Yes.

CLIVE: You didn't tell her …

LUCY: I didn't tell her anything. I just said I wanted to see her. She's coming down first thing tomorrow morning.

CLIVE: I see.

LUCY: (*Pulling on her gloves*) If Janet can't get to sleep or complains of a headache, give her one of those little white tablets, they're by the side of my bed.

CLIVE: Yes, all right. Where are you going?

LUCY: (*Impatiently*) I'm going out, that's all.

CLIVE: (*Stopping her*) Lucy …

LUCY: (*Turning*) Yes?

CLIVE: I'm worried about your mother. This is going to be quite a shock, you know.

LUCY: (*A shrug*) There's nothing we can do about it.

3

CLIVE:      Would you like me to talk to her?

LUCY:       (*A note of sarcasm*) What is it, Clive? Are you frightened she won't see your point of view?

CLIVE:      (*Suddenly angry*) Oh, for goodness sake – what does it matter whether she sees my point of view or not? I'm only trying to be helpful.

LUCY:       (*Facing him; tensely*) We've been over this a thousand times. Nothing you can say to mother, Laurence, or anyone else can make the slightest difference.

CLIVE:      (*Trying to control himself*) Lucy, will you please realise – will you please try to understand – I'm just as keen on this divorce as you are; but we don't have to be at each other's throats every five minutes!

LUCY:       Don't we? Oh, I know what you'd like, Clive! You'd like to dress the whole thing up; give it the   Hollywood      treatment. (*Socially*) "Clive and Lucy are splitting up, you know – but they're still <u>awfully</u> good friends ..."

CLIVE:      (*Impatiently*) Oh, for heaven's sake be sensible!

LUCY:       (*With emotion*) I don't feel sensible! I feel angry and hurt and intensely bitter about the whole business.

CLIVE:      And of course you blame me, completely?

*The telephone on the desk starts to ring.*

LUCY:       (*Facing him: emphasising her words with a repeated shake of the head*) Completely, Clive. Completely. Completely.

4

CLIVE: (*Turning towards the desk; exasperated*) Oh, my God! (*He picks up the telephone receiver*) Hello?

PELFORD: (*On the other end*) Is that Beacherscross 189?

CLIVE: Yes.

PELFORD: (*With a professional charm*) Good evening. This is Profile Limited …

CLIVE: (*Impatiently*) What?

PELFORD: Is that Mr Freeman?

CLIVE: Yes, it is.

PELFORD: Good evening, Mr Freeman. This is Profile Limited.

CLIVE: Who the hell are you? What do you want?

PELFORD: (*Unabashed*) We've arranged to take some photographs, Mr Freeman, and we were wondering if …

CLIVE: Wait a minute! Hold on. (*To LUCY, still exasperated*) Do you know anything about this? It's something to do with photographs …

LUCY: Yes, I do – and there's no need to be rude. (*She crosses and takes the receiver*) (*On phone*) Hello? This is Mrs Freeman.

PELFORD: Oh, good evening! This is Profile Limited. Will Thursday afternoon be convenient for you – about four o'clock?

LUCY: Yes, that'll do nicely, I'll expect you then.

PELFORD: Thank you, Mrs Freeman. Goodbye!

*LUCY replaces the receiver and as she does so, ANNA, the Austrian maid, enters.*

CLIVE: (*To LUCY*) What's all that about?

LUCY: It's nothing to do with you. I'm having some photographs taken.

5

CLIVE:     Of yourself?

LUCY:      Don't be stupid – of Janet. (*To ANNA*) Yes, what is it, Anna?

ANNA:      Mr Hudson is here, madam.

LUCY:      Show him into the study, Anna.

*ANNA nods and goes out.*

CLIVE:     Look, Lucy, what's the point of my seeing Laurence alone? He's your solicitor as well as mine. If we're going to go through with this you'll have to talk to him sooner or later. Why not tonight?

LUCY:      (*Hesitates; nodding*) Yes, all right. (*She starts to take off her gloves*)


CUT TO:   Outside Amberley the next morning.

*A Standard Bentley is parked outside the main door. CLIVE is putting a suitcase into the boot of the car. JANET, an attractive little girl of about ten, appears in the doorway with LUCY. JANET wears a beret and carries a wooden pencil box and an exercise book.*

CLIVE:     (*Pleasantly*) Come along, Janet – or you'll be late!

*JANET kisses her MOTHER and runs across to the car. CLIVE smiles at her and opens the car door. JANET climbs into the car and CLIVE crosses to the driving seat, ignoring LUCY. JANET smiles at LUCY who is still standing in the doorway. The car starts to move away.*


CUT TO:   *The car draws to a standstill outside the entrance to a Preparatory School. Children are going into the school. JANET climbs out of the car, waves to her FATHER, and goes down the drive leading to the school. CLIVE sits in the car, watching her. He looks faintly disturbed.*

6

CUT TO: Drawing Room at Amberley. About an hour later.

*MRS DENBY enters, followed by LUCY. MRS DENBY, LUCY'S MOTHER, is a smart yet homely woman in her early sixties. LUCY turns in the doorway and calls out to ANNA who is in the hall.*

LUCY:          Put my mother's case in the guest room, Anna, and then bring the coffee.

ANNA:          (*Off*) Yes, Mrs Freeman.

MRS DENBY: (*Nodding towards the hall*) She's still with you, then?

LUCY:          Yes, and she's much happier. She hardly mentions The Blue Danube these days.

*MRS DENBY sits on the settee and eases off one of her shoes.*

MRS DENBY: The garden's looking very nice, Lucy.

LUCY:          (*Helping herself to a cigarette*) We've done rather well this year. The rhododendrons have been lovely.

*A slight pause.*

MRS DENBY: I suppose Janet's at school?

LUCY:          (*Lighting the cigarette; her thoughts elsewhere*) Yes, she'll be back this afternoon.

MRS DENBY: How's Clive?

LUCY:          (*Hesitant*) He's quite well, considering. (*She turns and faces the settee*) Mother, there's something I've got to tell you.

MRS DENBY: (*Smiling*) I rather gathered that. You've been on tenterhooks ever since we left the station. What is it, Lucy?

LUCY:          Clive and I have decided to … (*She hesitates*)

MRS DENBY: Yes, dear?

7

LUCY:          … Well, we're going to split up, Mother –
               we're getting a divorce.
MRS DENBY: (*A moment; non-committal*) Oh. Oh, I see.
*A slight pause.*
LUCY:          You don't seem very surprised.
MRS DENBY: Should I be?
LUCY:          Well, you've always been very fond of
               Clive. I thought …
MRS DENBY: I'm very fond of you both, Lucy.
LUCY:          Yes, I know but – (*Faintly irritated*) Well,
               haven't you anything to say?
MRS DENBY: What would you like me to say, dear?
LUCY:          I thought this would be a shock to you.
               Both Clive and I thought that … Well, we
               were quite worried. We didn't know how
               you'd take it.
MRS DENBY: It's a pity you don't show the same
               consideration towards each other.
LUCY:          Now, Mother, I don't want a lecture!
MRS DENBY: That's just what you do want! You can
               cope with words, Lucy – you always
               have been able to, ever since you were a
               little girl. Well, I'm not going to argue
               with you. You're old enough to make your
               own mistakes.
*LUCY rises and stubs out her cigarette.*
*There is a pause.*
LUCY:          It's no use, Mother, we've tried to make a
               go of it. The last eighteen months have
               been sheer hell. We argue over everything
               – even little things that are completely
               unimportant. Oh, I know it's not always
               Clive's fault. More often than not it's
               mine, I suppose. But the fact remains …

8

MRS DENBY:  Clive shouldn't have left Prescott. I said so at the time and I still say it.

LUCY:       But that's nonsense! What's Prescott got to do with it?

MRS DENBY:  You were both happy when he was doing research. The moment he started on his own …

LUCY:       Oh, Mother, for goodness sake don't confuse the issue – haven knows it's confused enough! This hasn't anything to do with Clive leaving Prescott, or making money, or being a success, or anything like that. Something's happened to us – either to me, or to Clive, or to both of us, perhaps. We don't feel the same towards each other. When that happens you just can't go on. It's no use.

MRS DENBY:  Have you tried?

LUCY:       Yes, of course. I've told you, this last year has been absolutely hell. For Clive as well, for both of us.

*ANNA enters, carrying a tray with coffee.*

ANNA:       (*Pleased to see MRS DENBY*) Good morning, Mrs Denby. It's very nice to see you again.

MRS DENBY: Thank you, Anna. How have you been keeping?

ANNA:       Very well, I hope, Mrs Denby. (*Puzzled*) Is that right – I hope?

MRS DENBY:  (*With a little smile, but her thoughts elsewhere*) Yes, that's right.

*ANNA puts the tray down and hands MRS DENBY a cup of coffee.*

MRS DENBY:  (*Taking the cup*) Thank you, Anna.

9

*LUCY walks across to the tray and picks up a cup of coffee. She looks across at her Mother, obviously puzzled by her attitude.*

CUT TO: Outside the entrance to Amberley. Night.
*A police car is parked outside the main entrance. CLIVE drives up, gets out of the Bentley, stares at the police car in surprise and goes into the house.*

CUT TO: Drawing Room at Amberley.
*LUCY, MRS DENBY, A UNIFORMED POLICE SERGEANT (SERGEANT BROOKS) and a PLAIN CLOTHES MAN (DETECTIVE INSPECTOR KENTON) are present. LUCY and MRS DENBY are obviously very distressed. KENTON is on the telephone, talking to the local operator. The INSPECTOR is a quiet, well-educated man in his late thirties.*

KENTON: ...Well, keep trying that number for the next quarter of an hour. Then, if there's no reply, I want you to get through to ...

*He breaks off as CLIVE enters the room.*

KENTON: It's all right, Operator. Cancel the call.

*He replaces the receiver.*

CLIVE: (*Puzzled*) What is it? What's happened?
LUCY: (*Quickly, a note of desperation in her voice*) Where's Janet?
CLIVE: (*Surprised*) Janet? Isn't she here – in bed?
LUCY: (*Tensely*) Clive, where's Janet? Where have you taken her?
CLIVE: (*Suddenly annoyed*) What do you mean – where have I taken her? (*To KENTON*) What is this? What's going on?

MRS DENBY: Janet's disappeared … She didn't return from school … We thought perhaps you'd picked her up, Clive.

CLIVE: (*Stunned*) Why, no! I haven't seen Janet. Not since this morning … (*Suddenly*) Good God, you mean to say no one's seen her? … Why, it's nearly midnight!

KENTON: I'm Inspector Kenton, sir. We've been trying to get in touch with you.

CLIVE: Yes, I realise that. I've been to the theatre. I didn't leave Town until …

LUCY: (*Overwrought, turning on him*) You said you were going to the club! When you left the house this morning you distinctly said …

MRS DENBY: Lucy, please! (*To CLIVE*) No one seems to have seen Janet – not since she said goodbye to Miss Calthorpe at four o'clock this afternoon.

CLIVE: (*To LUCY*) But didn't you meet her? You usually do.

LUCY: (*Desperately worried, nodding towards MRS DENBY*) We were talking and didn't realise the time. Miss Calthorpe walked with her as far as the bus stop. (*Defensively*) Well, it's not the first time; she's come home before on her own …

CLIVE: Have you phoned the Gibsons?

LUCY: Yes. The Gibsons, the Harpers, Mary Conway, everybody!

CLIVE: What about the school?

KENTON: (*Nodding*) We've been on to the school. The headmistress confirms she left

11

with Miss Calthorpe. It's obviously true because one of the other little girls saw …

*He is interrupted by the ringing of the telephone. SERGEANT BROOKS is stood near the telephone and immediately picks up the receiver. The others instinctively turn towards him.*

BROOKS: (*On phone*) Hello? Beacherscross 189.

WILLIAMS: (*On the other end*) Is that you, Sergeant?

BROOKS: Yes. Hold on, Williams. (*To KENTON*) It's Williams, sir.

*KENTON takes the telephone receiver.*

KENTON: (*On phone*) Hello, Williams! Any news?

WILLIAMS: Yes, sir. (*Quietly*) I'm afraid it's not very good.

*KENTON glances across at LUCY and CLIVE.*

KENTON: (*Quietly*) What do you mean?

WILLIAMS: A woman called Mrs Hughes saw her at a quarter past seven …

KENTON: Where?

WILLIAMS: At Kingsdown. That's near Henshaw Wood.

KENTON: That's twenty miles from here.

WILLIAMS: Yes, I know.

KENTON: Was she alone?

WILLIAMS: No, there was a man with her. We've got a description, but it's pretty vague, I'm afraid.

KENTON: Where are you? Where are you speaking from?

WILLIAMS: I'm in a box at Kingsdown, sir. We're just going to search the Wood.

KENTON: Right! You know the Fox and Goose – that's the pub near the pond on the far side?

12

WILLIAMS:      Yes.

KENTON:        I'll meet you there in an hour.

WILLIAMS:      Very good, sir!

*KENTON replaces the receiver.*

LUCY:          (*Tensely*) Have they found her?

KENTON:        (*Calmly; non-committal*) No. No, not yet,
               Mrs Freeman, but apparently someone saw
               her in Kingsdown just after seven o'clock.

MRS DENBY:     Kingsdown?

CLIVE:         Why, that must be twenty miles away!

KENTON:        Yes, I know, sir. Have you any friends or
               relatives in that part of the country?

LUCY:          No.

CLIVE:         (*Looking at the INSPECTOR*) Was she
               alone?

*KENTON ignores the question and turns towards LUCY.*

KENTON:        Try not to worry, Mrs Freeman. We'll do
               everything we can. (*To CLIVE*) I'll be in
               touch with you the moment there's any
               news.

CLIVE:         Where are you going now?

KENTON:        (*A momentary hesitation*) I'm going to
               Kingsdown, sir.

CLIVE:         I'm coming with you!

*CLIVE picks up his hat from the settee and follows the
INSPECTOR to the door.*


CUT TO:   Drawing room of Amberley.

*The clock on the mantelpiece says it is four o'clock in the
morning. LUCY is alone, slowly pacing up and down the
room. She is smoking a cigarette and looks desperately
worried and on edge. An ash tray on the centre table is full
of half smoked cigarettes. ANNA enters. She is wearing a
dressing gown over her nightdress.*

ANNA:       Can I get you anything, madam?

LUCY:       No. No, thank you, Anna. You should be in bed. You should have been in bed hours ago.

ANNA:       I've been getting Mrs Denby a glass of hot milk.

LUCY:       Is she all right now?

ANNA:       Yes, but she's been very sick, I'm afraid.

LUCY:       (*Nodding*) It's nerves. She can't help it. She's always like that when she's worried.

ANNA:       What do you think's happened to Janet, Mrs Freeman?

*Sound of the front door opening and closing.*

LUCY:       (*On edge*) We don't know what's happened, Anna.

ANNA:       I remember long before the war there was a little girl in Saltzburg and one day …

*She breaks off as CLIVE enters. He looks tense and worried.*

LUCY:       (*Quickly*) Is there any news?

CLIVE:      (*Shaking his head*) No … (*To ANNA*) Anna, d'you think you could make me some coffee – black coffee?

ANNA:       Of course, Mr Freeman. Of course …

*She goes out.*

LUCY:       What's happened?

CLIVE:      We've been searching Kingsdown, Henshaw Wood – the whole district. There's no sign of her.

*LUCY turns away, obviously distressed. CLIVE sinks down onto the arm of the settee.*

CLIVE:      They're going to ring, if there's any news.

LUCY:       Clive, what d'you think's happened?

CLIVE:      I don't know, Lucy.

14

LUCY:     What about the woman who was supposed to have seen her?

CLIVE:    Her name's Hughes. She lives in a cottage near Henshaw Wood.

LUCY:     Well, did she see her?

CLIVE:    Yes, I think so.

*He looks across at LUCY and rises from the settee. He is obviously very worried.*

CLIVE:    It was about a quarter past seven. Mrs Hughes was in her garden and Janet walked past the cottage.

LUCY:     Was she alone?

CLIVE:    (*Hesitant*) No. There was a man with her, a dishevelled looking chap. The police have got details. They're trying to locate him.

LUCY:     (*Tensely*) Who was it, Clive?

CLIVE:    (*Rising and moving across towards the window*) I don't know. (*Restlessly*) This Mrs Hughes is very old. She must be nearly eighty. I just don't know whether she's a reliable witness or not.

LUCY:     But you said she <u>saw</u> Janet.

CLIVE:    Well, she described her. She said the little girl was wearing a beret and a blue gymslip. She noticed the exercise book and the pencil case.

LUCY:     But they're all dressed like that. They all carry exercise books and …

CLIVE:    (*Interrupting*) Yes, I know, but – I don't think there's any doubt about it, Lucy. It was Janet.

*He stands for the moment looking out of the window.*

CLIVE:    Where's your mother?

LUCY:     She's upstairs. She's been sick. You know Mother. (*A moment*) You say they're going to telephone?

15

CLIVE:     (*Standing with his back to her*) Yes. The Inspector said he'd get through if there was any news. He's a very decent chap, he's doing everything he can.

*LUCY crosses to the table and takes a cigarette from the box. There is a pause.*

LUCY:     Why did you come back?

*CLIVE shrugs. He does not turn from the window.*

LUCY:     You said this morning you were going to stay at the club.

CLIVE:     Yes. I know I did.

LUCY:     What made you change your mind?

*CLIVE turns and points towards the writing bureau.*

CLIVE:     I left something in the desk – a report on the Zeissman test. I needed it at the office.

LUCY:     Was that your only reason?

CLIVE:     What do you mean?

LUCY:     Was that the only reason you came back tonight?

*As LUCY speaks the telephone rings. LUCY and CLIVE instinctively turn towards it then CLIVE springs forward and picks up the receiver. LUCY stands by his side.*

CLIVE:     (*On phone*) Hello … Hello? …

*There is no voice on the other end of the line.*

CLIVE:     Hello! …

*The receiver at the other end is replaced and we hear the dialling tone.*

LUCY:     (*Quickly*) What's happened?

CLIVE:     They've rung off …

LUCY:     (*Astonished*) But why should they do that? (*Quickly*) Put the receiver down, they'll get through again!

*CLIVE replaces the receiver. They stand watching the telephone. After a pause, the telephone rings again.*

16

*CLIVE snatches up the receiver.*

CLIVE:     Hello? … Hello? …

LUCY:      (*Tensely*) Clive, what is it? What's happening?

CLIVE:     (*Impatiently tapping the receiver*) Hello!

*The receiver is replaced at the other end and the dialling tone returns.*

CLIVE:         They've rung off again!

LUCY:          Is it the phone?

CLIVE:         (*Dialling the Operator*) I don't think so.

*The ringing tone rings out and the Operator answers.*

OPERATOR:   Can I help you?

CLIVE:         Miss, there's someone trying to get through to this number, it's an urgent call …

OPERATOR:   Well, what seems to be the trouble?

CLIVE:         (*Impatiently*) I don't know what the trouble is … We keep getting the dialling tone …

OPERATOR:   There's no one on the line at the moment. I should replace the receiver.

*CLIVE looks desperate and undecided. Then he replaces the receiver.*

LUCY:          What are you going to do?

CLIVE:         (*Hand on receiver*) We'll wait a few minutes. If he doesn't ring, I'll get through to the police station.

LUCY:          (*Nodding*) Yes, all right.

*They stand looking at the telephone. Suddenly it rings again. CLIVE keeps his hand on the receiver but doesn't lift it. The ringing continues. He looks at LUCY, then raises the receiver.*

CLIVE:         Hello? …

*There is no voice on the other end of the line.*

CLIVE:         Hello? … (*Angrily*) Hello!

17

*The receiver at the other end is replaced. We hear the dialling tone again.*

LUCY:       Have they rung off again?

CLIVE:      Yes … (*He looks at LUCY thoughtfully*) I don't think this is the police.

LUCY:       What do you mean?

CLIVE:      (*Slowly*) I think someone's doing this deliberately …

*He looks at the receiver then slowly replaces it.*

CUT TO:   The front page of a national daily newspaper. There is a photograph of JANET FREEMAN on the front page. The newspaper headline reads: "Have you seen Janet Freeman?"

CUT TO:   The front page of a second daily newspaper. A large photograph illustrates the search party in Henshaw Wood. The headline reads: "Janet Freeman 10 days search continues".

CUT TO:   The office of LAURENCE HUDSON, in the Strand, London, WC2. This is a lawyer's office, furnished with taste and a certain degree of fastidiousness. LAURENCE HUDSON is sitting behind his kidney-shaped desk, writing a letter. He is about thirty-five or six: a distinguished looking man with a liking for good clothes. There is a flower in a narrow glass vase on his desk. He finishes the letter, blots the notepaper and finally puts the letter into an envelope. His secretary, URSULA WAYNE, enters. She carries a notebook.

LAURENCE:  (*Looking up*) Ursula, I want you to take this letter round to the Probate Office. It's in Chancery Lane.

URSULA:    Yes, Mr Hudson.

LAURENCE: Do it straight away. It's important. (*Consulting his pocket watch*) I shan't be here when you get back. Finish the letters and I'll sign them tomorrow morning.

URSULA: (*None too pleased*) Very well. (*She turns towards the door and then remembers something*) Oh, there's a Superintendent Wilde to see you.

LAURENCE: Superintendent Wilde?

URSULA: Yes.

LAURENCE: A police Superintendent?

URSULA: Yes, he's from Scotland Yard.

LAURENCE: (*A momentary hesitation*) Very well, Ursula, I'll see him straight away.

*He looks thoughtful as URSULA leaves. He takes out a bunch of keys and locks a drawer in his desk. He then rises to greet SUPERINTENDENT WILDE.*

LAURENCE: Come along in, Superintendent. (*Indicates a chair facing his desk*) I hope I haven't kept you waiting.

WILDE: (*Taking seat*) Not at all, sir. It's very kind of you to see me at a moment's notice.

LAURENCE: (*Smiling*) If you'd been ten minutes later, you'd have missed me. I'm going out to Beacherscross this evening.

WILDE: (*Pleasantly*) Are you visiting Mr Freeman, sir?

LAURENCE: Yes, I am as a matter of fact. I'm his lawyer, you know.

WILDE: So I understand.

LAURENCE: Are you investigating the Freeman case?

WILDE: I'm interested in it, sir. That's why I wanted to see you.

LAURENCE:    (*Nodding*) I thought perhaps it was. (*He
             returns to his chair, facing the
             SUPERINTENDENT*) I couldn't imagine
             any other reason.

WILDE:       You told Inspector Kenton that you saw
             Mr and Mrs Freeman the night before the
             child disappeared.

LAURENCE:    Yes.

WILDE:       That was on the 19$^{th}$ …

LAURENCE:    It was a fortnight yesterday.

WILDE:       (*Nodding*) That's right. (*Pleasantly, yet a
             rather sudden question*) Why did you see
             them, sir? Did Mr Freeman send for you?

LAURENCE:    I've told you. I'm Clive Freeman's lawyer.
             We see a great deal of each other. I'm
             actually on the Board of one of his
             Companies.

WILDE:       (*Thoughtfully*) Yes, that's what you told
             the Inspector. (*Smiling*) But it doesn't
             answer my question.

LAURENCE:    What was your question?

WILDE:       I asked you why you saw Mr and Mrs
             Freeman on the evening of September the
             19$^{th}$.

LAURENCE:    Clive sent for me. He had a problem, and
             he wanted my advice.

WILDE:       What was the problem?

LAURENCE:    Oh, really, Inspector! Will it help you to
             find Janet if you know why her father
             consulted his  lawyer the night before she
             disappeared?

WILDE:       (*Non-committal*) It might, sir.

*LAURENCE rises and looks at WILDE for a moment.*

20

| | |
|---|---|
| LAURENCE: | I suppose you've been questioning the tradespeople, listening to gossip. |
| WILDE: | We've heard one or two rumours – yes, sir. |
| LAURENCE: | Mr and Mrs Freeman haven't been getting on very well together – there was some talk of a divorce and they wanted my advice. |
| WILDE: | I see. Was there a third party involved? |
| LAURENCE: | No, no, no. Nothing like that, I assure you. It was simply that – well – they just hadn't been hitting it off. |
| WILDE: | I understand. Thank you, sir. (*Rises*) That's all I wanted to know. |
| LAURENCE: | Have you made any progress – is there any news? |
| WILDE: | (*Shaking his head*) I'm afraid not. We're exactly where we were a fortnight ago. |
| LAURENCE: | Mrs Freeman's been very ill, you know. On the verge of a nervous breakdown. |
| WILDE: | So I understand. How long have you known the Freemans, sir? |
| LAURENCE: | About six years. I met Clive just after he left Prescott. |
| WILDE: | What made him leave Prescott, sir – do you know? |
| LAURENCE: | Oh, various things. He got tired of research – wanted to make more money – wanted to start a business of his own. He's done remarkably well, you know. |
| WILDE: | Yes, so I believe. (*He holds out his hand*) Sorry to have troubled you, Mr Hudson. |
| LAURENCE: | (*Shaking hands*) That's all right, Superintendent. |

WILDE:        (*Turning as he reaches the door, an afterthought*) Oh, by the way, do you happen to know anyone called Nelson?

LAURENCE:  Nelson? I don't think so. What initials?

WILDE:        I don't know his initials, sir. Just Mr Nelson.

LAURENCE:  (*Shaking his head*) No, I don't think I know  anyone called Nelson …

WILDE:        (*Smiling*) It's not important, sir. Give Mr and Mrs Freeman my regards.

LAURENCE:  Yes, I will certainly.

*LAURENCE opens the door and with a nod WILDE goes out. LAURENCE turns to his desk, glances at his watch, then turns and takes a bowler hat and a rolled umbrella out of a corner cupboard. He takes the flower out of the vase and puts it in his buttonhole. As he picks up the hat and umbrella the telephone rings.*

LAURENCE:  (*On phone*) Hello?

GIRL:          There's a call for you, Mr Hudson.

LAURENCE:  Thank you.

GIRL:          Just a moment, sir.

*A slight pause and there is a connection from the switchboard.*

LAURENCE:  Hello?

PELFORD:    Is that Mr Laurence Hudson?

LAURENCE:  Yes – speaking.

PELFORD:    Good afternoon, Mr Hudson, I understand Mr Freeman's a client of yours – Mr Clive Freeman?

LAURENCE:  Yes, he is, but if you're a newspaper reporter, I'm afraid …

PELFORD:    (*Quickly, a shade appalled by the suggestion*) No, no, no, I'm nothing like that, I assure you! Heaven forbid!

22

| | |
|---|---|
| LAURENCE: | Well, who are you? What is it you want? |
| PELFORD: | I want you to deliver a message. Tell Mrs Freeman to look at the exercise book. |
| LAURENCE: | What exercise book? |
| PELFORD: | Just the exercise book, Mr Hudson – she'll understand. (*He replaces the receiver*) |
| LAURENCE: | What do you mean? What are you talking about … (*Realising the line has been cleared*) Hello? Hello! (*He looks at the receiver in his hand*) |

CUT TO: LUCY's dressing room. Amberley. Late afternoon. The curtains are drawn. There is a divan bed, dressing table, built-in wardrobes etc. The door is closed, a blanket is wedged between the carpet and the foot of the door. LUCY is lying on a rug in front of the gas fire which is turned on. After a moment, voices can be heard on the landing outside.

| | |
|---|---|
| CLIVE: | (*Off*) It's coming from here, Anna – from the dressing room! (*Nearer the door*) Are you sure Mrs Freeman's out? |
| ANNA: | (*Off*) Ja … she told me she was going into the village. |
| CLIVE: | (*Off*) When was that? |
| ANNA: | (*Off*) About ten minutes ago … |

*CLIVE tries the door handle, finds the door locked.*

| | |
|---|---|
| CLIVE: | (*Off, calling*) Lucy! Lucy, are you in there? |
| ANNA: | (*Off, perturbed*) Is the door locked, Mr Freeman? |
| CLIVE: | (*Off, throwing his weight against the door*) Yes, it is … |

*He continues to throw his weight against the door until the lock breaks and the door falls open. CLIVE is wearing a*

23

*hat and overcoat and he stands for a moment in the doorway taking in the scene, suddenly he covers his mouth with a handkerchief, rushes across to LUCY and turns off the gas fire. ANNA runs across the room, throws back the curtains and opens the window. CLIVE throws down his hat and then takes hold of LUCY and lifts her onto the divan.*

CLIVE:    (*To ANNA*) Get Dr Wesley – the number's downstairs!

*ANNA nods and rushes out of the room.*

CLIVE:    (*To LUCY, tensely*) Lucy … (*He slaps her face*) Lucy!

*LUCY opens her eyes and looks up at CLIVE.*

LUCY:    (*Weakly, the words barely distinguishable*) Where's Janet? What's happened to … Janet?

CLIVE:    Lucy, listen! Have you taken anything? Did you take any tablets?

LUCY:    (*Dazed*) Is there any news? Where's Janet? …

*CLIVE takes hold of her shoulder, shakes her.*

CLIVE:    Lucy, listen to me! Did you take anything – did you take any tablets?

*LUCY stares at him for a moment, she is slowly recovering.*

LUCY:    What did you say?

CLIVE:    (*Quietly*) I said, did you take anything, Lucy – any tablets.

LUCY:    (*Shaking her head*) No. No, I … didn't … think of it …

*CLIVE sits down on the end of the bed, relieved. He stares down at LUCY then suddenly puts his hand across his eyes, he is tired and weary.*

LUCY:    (*Near to tears*) I'm sorry, Clive. I was so worried … I'm sorry … I'm sorry, Clive …

CLIVE: (*After a moment, looking up*) I've told Anna to get Dr Wesley.

LUCY: There's no need … I'll be all right now. Just get me a drink of water …

*CLIVE looks at her, hesitates, then nods and rises from the bed.*


CUT TO: The Drawing Room. Two hours later.

*DETECTIVE INSPECTOR KENTON is sitting in an armchair, alone. There is an attaché case on the floor by the side of his chair. He glances at his wristlet watch as CLIVE enters from the hall.*

CLIVE: I'm sorry to have kept you waiting, Inspector. My wife hasn't been very well this afternoon.

KENTON: (*Interrupting him*) Oh, I hope it's nothing serious, sir?

*LUCY appears in the doorway behind CLIVE. She is wearing a dressing gown and looks distinctly pale and worried.*

CLIVE: No, I don't think so. I think she's just feeling the strain of the last week or two … (*He realises LUCY is behind him and turns*) Lucy, I told you not to come down!

LUCY: I'm all right. I'm perfectly all right now. Don't fuss – please don't fuss, Clive.

KENTON: I'm sorry you haven't been very well, Mrs Freeman.

LUCY: (*Tensely*) I'm all right, Inspector. I'm perfectly all right now.

*KENTON looks at LUCY obviously curious then turns towards CLIVE.*

CLIVE: Well, Inspector?

LUCY: What's happened? Is there any news? Have you found Janet?

KENTON: No, Mrs Freeman, but we found these early this afternoon. Do you recognise them?

*He takes an exercise book and a wooden pencil box out of the attaché case.*

LUCY: (*Tensely*) Yes … yes, they're Janet's! Where did you find them?

*KENTON looks at LUCY, then across at CLIVE.*

KENTON: Well, curiously enough, in Henshaw Wood.

CLIVE: What do you mean – curiously enough?

KENTON: During the past fortnight, we've been through that wood with a toothcomb, sir.

CLIVE: Well?

KENTON: Well, this afternoon one of my men found these articles in a bush not far from the main road. We've searched those bushes before, sir, not once, but half a dozen times.

CLIVE: I don't see what you're getting at?

LUCY: (*Pointing to the pencil case*) You mean – someone put these things there, quite recently?

KENTON: (*Quietly*) Yes, Mrs Freeman.

CLIVE: But why should they do that?

KENTON: Well, either they wanted to dispose of them – in which case why pick such a conspicuous spot? – or they particularly wanted us to find them.

CLIVE: (*Shaking his head*) That doesn't make sense to me. I'm sorry, Inspector, it's my bet they've been there all the time and they've been overlooked.

KENTON: No, sir, that's not possible.

CLIVE: Oh, come now, Inspector! None of us are infallible.

KENTON: I know that, but aren't you overlooking something? (*He picks up the exercise book and*

26

*hands it to CLIVE*) … Would you say that book was damp, sir?

*CLIVE rubs his hand across the exercise book.*

CLIVE: (*Shaking his head*) No.

KENTON: But it rained last night – quite heavily in fact.

*CLIVE looks at the exercise book.*

CLIVE: (*Thoughtfully*) Yes. Yes, you're quite right – it did.

LUCY: (*To KENTON*) Inspector, what does this mean? Do you think …?

KENTON: (*Quietly, interrupting her*) I don't know what it means, Mrs Freeman, but – well, it's a start at any rate, so far as we're concerned.

CLIVE: Have you told Superintendent Wilde about this?

KENTON: Yes.

CLIVE: What did he say?

KENTON: He made no comment. (*A moment, remembering*) Oh, incidentally, he asked me if, by any chance, you knew anyone called Nelson.

CLIVE: Nelson?

KENTON: Yes. Mr Nelson.

*CLIVE looks at LUCY, who shakes her head.*

CLIVE: No.

LUCY: Who's Mr Nelson?

KENTON: I don't know, Mrs Freeman. I was simply told to ask the question. (*He points to the exercise book and pencil case*) You're quite sure these do belong to Janet?

LUCY: Yes, I'm positive.

KENTON: There's no name on the exercise book and there's nothing on the pencil case …

27

LUCY:          Yes, I know, but they're Janet's, I'm sure
               of it.
KENTON:        Could anybody else identify them?
LUCY:          Well ... Miss Calthorpe, I suppose ...
               Janet's teacher ...
CLIVE:         She's calling round this evening ... (*To
               LUCY*) She telephoned this morning and
               said something about a puppet ... I
               couldn't make head or tail of it, so I asked
               her to call round.
LUCY:          Yes, I know what it is.
KENTON:        Well, you might ask Miss Calthorpe to
               take a look at these things. If she doesn't
               think they are Janet's ask her to give me a
               ring.

*ANNA enters.*

CLIVE:         What is it, Anna?
ANNA:          Mr Hudson's arrived, sir.
CLIVE:         Oh, ask him in.

*ANNA goes out.*

KENTON:        (*Indicating the pencil case and exercise
               book*) Unless I hear from Miss Calthorpe,
               I'll pick these things up tomorrow
               morning.
LUCY:          Inspector ...
KENTON:        Yes, Mrs Freeman?
LUCY:          Tell me, quite honestly ... do you think
               you'll ever find Janet?

*KENTON hesitates, looks at LUCY, then across at CLIVE.*

KENTON:        Yes, I do. I do, Mrs Freeman but – don't
               ask me why I think so. It's just ... a
               feeling I've got. (*He turns towards the
               door, then hesitates, looks at CLIVE*)

|  |  |
|---|---|
|  | Incidentally, I take it no one's contacted you, Mr Freeman? |
| CLIVE: | (*Faintly surprised by the question*) Why, no – no-one. Except the newspapers, of course. |

*LAURENCE HUDSON enters. He hesitates when he sees KENTON.*

| KENTON: | (*To LAURENCE*) Good evening, sir. |
|---|---|
| LAURENCE: | Oh, good evening, Inspector. |
| KENTON: | (*To LUCY*) Goodnight, Mrs Freeman. |
| LUCY: | Goodnight, Inspector. |

(*KENTON goes out with CLIVE*)

| LAURENCE: | (*To LUCY*) What did the Inspector want, Lucy? Is there any news? |
|---|---|
| LUCY: | (*Indicating the exercise book and case*) They found these this afternoon. |
| LAURENCE: | Where? |
| LUCY: | In Henshaw Wood. |

*LAURENCE crosses and picks up the exercise book.*

| LAURENCE: | (*A note of tenseness in his voice*) Is this Janet's? |
|---|---|
| LUCY: | (*Looking at him, surprised by his tone of voice*) Yes. |
| LAURENCE: | Are you sure? |
| LUCY: | Yes. She was carrying it the day she disappeared. The exercise book and the pencil box. |

*LAURENCE stares at the exercise book, obviously puzzled.*

| LUCY: | (*Moving towards LAURENCE*) Laurence, why are you looking like that? |
|---|---|

*LAURENCE looks up as CLIVE enters.*

| LAURENCE: | (*Slowly*) Clive, Lucy – I've got some news for you. |
|---|---|

29

CLIVE:          What do you mean?

LUCY:           Laurence, what is it?

*LAURENCE moves towards LUCY and CLIVE, still holding the exercise book.*

LAURENCE:       A man telephoned me this afternoon, just as I was leaving the office. He said, "Tell Mrs Freeman to look at the exercise book."

CLIVE:          Look at the exercise book!

*He crosses, takes the book out of LAURENCE's hand and glances through the pages.*

LUCY:           (*To LAURENCE*) What else did he say?

LAURENCE:       He didn't say anything else. Before I could question him, he rang off.

CLIVE:          (*Tensely*) When did this happen?

LAURENCE:       Just before I left the office – about five o'clock.

*CLIVE moves towards the door.*

CLIVE:          We'd better get hold of the Inspector. He ought to know about this …

LUCY:           Clive, wait a minute! (*To LAURENCE*) You say this man said … "Tell Mrs Freeman to look at the exercise book" …

LAURENCE:       Yes. I didn't know what the devil he meant. I still don't, if it comes to that.

CLIVE:          (*Looking at the exercise book*) There's nothing here … It's just a spelling book … Words copied from the blackboard, I should imagine.

*We see an open page of the exercise book in CLIVE's hand. There is a page of words written in a child's handwriting. The words are: Flag, Flaggon, Flame, Flash, Flamingo, Flatter.*

*CLIVE flicks the pages of the book and we see another page of words written by Janet. The words are: Gauge, Gavotte, Gazelle, General, Gentle.*

CLIVE:       I don't see what on earth he was talking about – there's nothing in here.

*LUCY takes the book from CLIVE and examines it.*

LAURENCE:  Is it Janet's handwriting?

LUCY:        (*Looking at the book*) Yes …

LAURENCE:  All of it – every page?

*LUCY turns the pages of the book. CLIVE moves to her side and looks at the book with LUCY.*

LUCY:        (*Nodding*) Yes, it's all the same.

*CLIVE takes the book from LUCY, and obviously puzzled examines it again. ANNA enters.*

ANNA:        Excuse me, madam …

LUCY:        Yes, what is it, Anna?

ANNA:        There's a Miss Calthorpe. She says she spoke to Mr Freeman this morning and he said …

CLIVE:       (*Looking up, interrupting ANNA*) Yes, that's all  right, Anna – ask her to come in.

*ANNA goes out.*

LAURENCE:  (*Puzzled*) Who's Miss Calthorpe? I seem to  know that name …

LUCY:        She's Janet's teacher. You met her at the Garden Fete last year.

LAURENCE:  Oh, yes, of course. (*A sudden thought*) Clive, if she's Janet's teacher, it might be a good idea …

CLIVE:       (*Forestalling him*) Yes, that's what I was thinking …

*ANNA enters with MISS CALTHORPE. RUTH CALTHORPE might be any age between forty and fifty: she is good looking in a faded, genteel kind of way.*

RUTH: Good evening, Mrs Freeman. I do hope I'm not intruding.

LUCY: No, we've been expecting you, Miss Calthorpe. I think you've met Mr Hudson before.

LAURENCE: (*Pleasantly*) Yes, we've met before, Miss Calthorpe.

*RUTH crosses and shakes hands with him.*

RUTH: Why, yes, of course. How very nice to see you again. (*To CLIVE*) I caught a glimpse of a police car as I came down the lane. I wondered if perhaps …

CLIVE: (*Shaking his head*) No, I'm afraid there's no news, Miss Calthorpe.

RUTH: Oh. Oh, I'm sorry. (*Faintly embarrassed*) Well, I really must apologise for troubling you like this, but … Janet had a puppet … she borrowed it a little while ago and …

LUCY: Yes, I think I know the one you mean. (*To ANNA, who is still standing in the doorway*) Anna, you know the toybox in Janet's room?

ANNA: Yes, Mrs Freeman?

LUCY: I think you'll find a puppet in there … It's on the top near the dolls' house.

ANNA: Ja … Ja, I know the one you mean.

LUCY: Well, fetch it down please, Anna.

*ANNA nods and goes out.*

LAURENCE: Are you giving a puppet show, Miss Calthorpe?

RUTH:        Well about a month ago we decided to give one, for Charity, you know – the Felton Girls' Home – then when Janet ... Well, we had to cancel it, and now the Headmistress has suddenly decided to go ahead again. It's all rather difficult, especially with the exams coming along, but ... (*To LUCY, apologetically*) Of course I'll let you have the puppet back again, Mrs Freeman, the moment the show is over.

LUCY:        Oh, that doesn't matter. I think it belongs to the school, anyway.

RUTH:        Well, it does strictly speaking, of course, but all the young children were told that they could keep ... (*She breaks off, staring at the exercise book in CLIVE's hand*)

CLIVE:       I see you're looking at the exercise book, Miss Calthorpe.

RUTH:        Why, yes! Is that Janet's?

CLIVE:       Well, we think so. What do you think, Miss Calthorpe?

*CLIVE hands RUTH the exercise book. She starts to examine it.*

RUTH:        (*Looking up*) Why, yes! This is Janet's ... It's her spelling book ... But I thought she had this book with her the day she ...

CLIVE:       (*Interrupting her*) She did. It was found this afternoon together with the pencil case.

RUTH:        (*Stunned*) Oh. Oh, I see ...

*RUTH looks at LUCY, undecided whether this is good news or not.*

CLIVE:          You're quite sure that it is Janet's?
RUTH:           (*Looking at the book again*) Yes … Yes,
                I'm positive. (*Turning over the pages of
                the exercise book*) It's her handwriting.
                You see, we write the words on a
                blackboard and then the whole class
                copies them … down … so … that … (*She
                hesitates, staring at the book*) … That's
                very odd …
CLIVE:          (*Watching RUTH*) What is it?
LAURENCE:       What is it, Miss Calthorpe?
RUTH:           Well … Janet's written down several
                words we haven't … had …
LUCY:           What do you mean?
CLIVE:          What do you mean – words you haven't
                had?
RUTH:           (*Pointing to the book*) She's written
                several words beginning with P. We
                haven't reached the letter P yet, Mr
                Freeman. You see, we've been going
                through the alphabet … As a matter of
                fact, when Janet … left ... we'd only
                reached M.

*LAURENCE takes the book from Ruth and looks at it.*

LAURENCE:       Are you sure she wrote this page?
RUTH:           Well, it's the same handwriting …
CLIVE:          (*A note of tenseness in his voice; to
                LAURENCE*) What are the words?
LAURENCE:       (*Reading from the book*) People, pictures,
                photographs, profile.
CLIVE:          (*Suddenly*) Photographs? Profile? (*He
                looks across at LUCY*)
LAURENCE:       Does that mean anything to you, Clive?

CLIVE: Why, yes! The day before Janet disappeared someone ...

*He breaks off as ANNA enters carrying the puppet.*

ANNA: (*Holding out the puppet*) Is this the one you want, Mrs Freeman?

LUCY: Yes ... (*To RUTH*) That's it, isn't it, Miss Calthorpe?

RUTH: Yes, thank you very much.

*RUTH crosses to the door and takes the puppet from ANNA. ANNA smiles and goes out. CLIVE crosses to RUTH and holds out the exercise book.*

CLIVE: Miss Calthorpe, are you sure about this – are you quite sure Janet didn't write this page while she was at school?

RUTH: She couldn't have done, Mr Freeman. I've just explained to you – we haven't reached the letter P yet.

*CLIVE looks at her; gives a decisive nod.*

CLIVE: Thank you, Miss Calthorpe – you've been most helpful.

*RUTH looks at LUCY, then at CLIVE and LAURENCE. She is obviously puzzled.*

RUTH: Forgive me, but I don't know what this is all about.

CLIVE: I told Inspector Kenton you were calling, and he asked me to show you the exercise book. My wife was pretty sure it was Janet's, but the Inspector wanted to make absolutely sure.

RUTH: Oh, yes, it's Janet's all right, I recognised it at once. (*Shaking her head*) There's no doubt about it.

CLIVE: Thank you, Miss Calthorpe.

*RUTH hesitates, still puzzled, then turns towards LUCY.*

RUTH:      Goodbye, Mrs Freeman. I do hope you have
           some good news very soon.
LUCY:      Thank you.
RUTH:      (*To CLIVE and LUCY*) Goodbye.
CLIVE:      Goodbye, Miss Calthorpe.
LAURENCE: (*With a little bow*) Goodbye.
*RUTH crosses to the door carrying the puppet which
represents a sailor. She looks at the puppet as she reaches
the door, then turns and smiles at LUCY.*
RUTH:      (*To LUCY*) And thank you for Mr Nelson.
*LUCY, CLIVE and LAURENCE stare at her in
amazement.*
CLIVE:     (*Moving towards her*) Mr Nelson?
RUTH:      Yes – the puppet. (*She smiles and
           rearranges the hat on the puppet's head*)
           We always call him Mr Nelson.


# END OF EPISODE ONE

# EPISODE TWO

OPEN TO: The Drawing Room at Amberley.

*The puppet is in RUTH CALTHORPE's hand. As she speaks we see that LUCY, CLIVE and LAURENCE are all staring at her and the puppet.*

RUTH:        And thank you for Mr Nelson.

CLIVE:       Mr Nelson?

RUTH:        Yes – the puppet. (*She smiles and rearranges the hat on the puppet's head*) We always call him Mr Nelson.

CLIVE:       (*Hesitant; puzzled*) Why?

RUTH:        (*Surprised by the question*) I beg your pardon?

LAURENCE:    Why do you call him Mr Nelson?

RUTH:        (*Amused*) Because he's a sailor, Mr Hudson – that's why!

LAURENCE:    (*Hesitant*) Yes, I know, but – it seems an odd name for a puppet.

CLIVE:       (*Looking at LAURENCE*) Yes, that's what I thought.

RUTH:        Well, I'm afraid we just couldn't think of anything else. Oh, I believe someone did suggesting calling him Drake. (*Looking at the puppet*) But somehow, he doesn't look like a Mr Drake, does he? (*A moment*) Well, goodbye! I do hope you'll have some good news very soon.

CLIVE:       Thank you, Miss Calthorpe. Goodbye.

RUTH:        (*To LUCY*) No. No, it's quite all right, really, Mrs Freeman. I can see myself out.

*She smiles to LAURENCE and goes out into the hall. LUCY goes with her but returns almost immediately.*

CLIVE:       (*To LAURENCE*) You'd obviously heard that name before, Laurence?

LAURENCE:    Yes.

CLIVE:         When?

LAURENCE:    Well, oddly enough this afternoon. Superintendent Wilde called to see me. Just as he was leaving, he asked me if I knew anyone called Nelson.

CLIVE:         And do you?

LAURENCE:    Why, no.

LUCY:          (*To CLIVE*)    But what about the puppet – is that just a coincidence?

*CLIVE looks across at LAURENCE who gives a little shrug.*

LAURENCE:    I suppose it must be. (*Curious*) Clive, what was all that about the exercise book?

CLIVE:         (*Picks up the exercise book*) Yes, that's very odd. I just don't understand it.

LUCY:          What do you mean – what's odd about it?

CLIVE:         Well, first of all, the book was found this afternoon – in Henshaw Wood. The Inspector's convinced it was planted there, and I'm inclined to agree with him.

LAURENCE:    You think the man who telephoned me …

CLIVE:         I think the man who telephoned you knew perfectly well that we should see the exercise book. (*He holds up the book*) I think this is a definite invitation for us to get in touch with them    …

LUCY:          But get in touch with whom?

LAURENCE:    Exactly!

*CLIVE opens the exercise book.*

CLIVE:         (*Reading from the book*) People, Pictures, Photographs, Profile. That's Janet's handwriting but we know from what Miss Calthorpe's told us that she must have written those words <u>after</u> she disappeared, not before.

LAURENCE: (*Nodding*) Well?

CLIVE: The day Janet disappeared Lucy had a phone call from a firm called Profile, Ltd.

*LAURENCE looks across at LUCY.*

LAURENCE: Profile, Ltd?

LUCY: Yes, it's a photographer's. Run by a man called Pelford. He'd arranged to take some photographs of Janet. I fixed it up weeks ago.

CLIVE: Did you meet this Mr Pelford?

LUCY: No. We made the arrangements over the telephone.

*LAURENCE takes the exercise book from CLIVE and looks at the page.*

LAURENCE: Who told you about this firm in the first place?

LUCY: I think it was Lady Barstow. Yes, I'm sure it was. We were talking about photographs one day and she showed me some she'd had taken of her dogs. (*To CLIVE*) You know how she fusses over those Corgis. Well, we've never had any decent photographs of Janet, so I thought I'd do something about it.

LAURENCE: So you contacted Pelford?

LUCY: Yes. They were very busy at the time and he said he'd ring back later. (*To CLIVE*) That was the call you answered.

LAURENCE: Who is this Lady Barstow? Is she a friend of yours?

CLIVE:          She's a neighbour. She lives in that
                derelict old house next to the Riding
                School.

LAURENCE:       I think I've seen her. A rather horsey type
                of woman.

CLIVE:          (*Smiling*) I don't think she'd care for that
                very much. Doggy, yes, but definitely not
                horsey.

LUCY:           (*Pointing to the exercise book*) Clive, what
                do you make of all this? Do you think that
                …?

*CLIVE crosses to the telephone.*

CLIVE:          I think we ought to contact Kenton. This is
                too big a coincidence for my liking.

LUCY:           No, wait a minute! (*To LAURENCE*) Do
                you agree, Laurence? Do you think we
                ought to tell the    Inspector about this?

LAURENCE:       Why, yes, of course! What else can you
                do?

LUCY:           We can phone Pelford ourselves and see
                what he's got to say.

CLIVE:          (*Hesitating*) I think it's too risky, Lucy.

LUCY:           Isn't it a risk if we tell Kenton? (*Pointing
                to the exercise book*) Why do you think
                the word profile was put in the exercise
                book? For our benefit or the Inspector's?

CLIVE:          For our benefit. I've already said that.

LUCY:           Then I think we ought to get in touch with
                Pelford, not Kenton.

*CLIVE hesitates and looks across at LAURENCE.*

CLIVE:          I don't like it. If we're not perfectly frank
                with the police they're bound to think …

LUCY: (*On edge*) I don't care what they think! I'm not interested in the police! I'm interested in finding Janet.

CLIVE: (*Quietly*) We're both interested in that, Lucy. (*To LAURENCE*) What do you think, Laurence – you're the lawyer?

*LAURENCE looks at LUCY. He is obviously sympathetic, but he turns towards CLIVE.*

LAURENCE: If I were you, I'd tell the Inspector.

*CLIVE nods and starts to dial the number.*

CUT TO: The Drawing Room at Amberley.

*KENTON is facing CLIVE, LUCY and LAURENCE as he turns over the pages of the exercise book.*

KENTON: … I take it, from what you've told me, that Miss Calthorpe was quite certain about this – adamant, in fact?

CLIVE: Absolutely adamant. She said that when Janet disappeared, they hadn't even reached the letter M.

KENTON: Which means that this could only have been written after Janet disappeared.

CLIVE: Yes.

KENTON: Mrs Freeman, what do you know about this firm – Profile, Ltd.

LUCY: I don't know anything about them except that it's run by a man called Pelford.

KENTON: Why did you contact them in the first place?

LUCY: (*A shade irritated*) I've told you why. I wanted some photographs taken of Janet. Lady Barstow recommended them.

KENTON: Why did she recommend them – were you talking about photographs at the time?

LUCY: (*Still irritated*) Yes, of course.

KENTON: (*Firmly, but not unpleasantly*) Mrs Freeman, this may be very important. I'd like you to tell me exactly what Lady Barstow said.

LUCY: We were having coffee together one morning and she started talking about her dogs. She's very fond of her dogs, you know. She's got four or five Corgis.

*KENTON nods.*

LUCY: Well, she told me that she'd just had their photographs taken and she was absolutely delighted with them. I asked her who took the photographs and she said it was a London firm called Profile, Ltd. She said they were awfully good with animals and very young children.

KENTON: Go on.

LUCY: Well I thought about it for a day or two and then I – and then I telephoned them.

KENTON: How did you get the number – did Lady Barstow give it to you?

LUCY: (*Thoughtfully*) Yes, I believe she did.

KENTON: Go on, Mrs Freeman.

LUCY: Well, that's all. I spoke to Pelford, he said they were frightfully busy, but he'd ring back later and make an appointment. He did.

KENTON: Did you mention this to your husband at all?

LUCY: No.

KENTON: Why not?

LUCY: It wasn't important. (*Looks at CLIVE*) Besides, I don't tell my husband everything, Inspector.

*KENTON looks at LUCY, then across at LAURENCE.*

KENTON: Mr Hudson, this telephone call you received …

LAURENCE: Yes?

KENTON: What kind of voice was it?

LAURENCE: Oh, dear!

KENTON: Had the man an accent?

LAURENCE: No, but he was rather … Oh, it's difficult to say. Precise? Pedantic, perhaps …

CLIVE: (*To LAURENCE*) Self-satisfied?

LAURENCE: Yes. Yes, I think that's the best way to describe it.

KENTON: (*To CLIVE*) What made you say that, sir?

CLIVE: Well, that's how Pelford sounded – at least he did to me. Very sure of himself. Self-satisfied.

LAURENCE: Yes, that's it – exactly.

*KENTON looks at CLIVE. He is thoughtful. Then he turns to LUCY.*

KENTON: Mrs Freeman – do you happen to have a group photograph which includes Janet?

LUCY: Yes, I think so.

CLIVE: (*To LUCY*) There's the one she had taken at school …

KENTON: (*Nodding*) That's the sort of thing I mean. Could I see it?

LUCY: (*Puzzled*) Yes, of course. But the Superintendent's got at least half-a-dozen photographs of Janet. This one isn't very good, you know. You can hardly recognise her.

KENTON:      (*Interrupting*) That's all right, Mrs
             Freeman. I'd just like to have a look at it.

*LUCY crosses to the writing bureau, opens a drawer and
takes out an unframed photograph. ANNA enters.*

CLIVE:       What is it, Anna?

ANNA:        Lady Barstow's here, sir. She'd like to
             have a word with Mrs Freeman.

CLIVE:       Oh. (*To LUCY*) Are you expecting her?

LUCY:        No. (*To ANNA*) Ask her to wait in the
             study, Anna. Tell her I shan't be …

*She breaks off as BARBARA BARSTOW appears in the
doorway. BARBARA BARSTOW is a well-built forthright
woman in her early fifties. She wears tweeds and flat-
heeled shoes.*

BARBARA:     Oh, good Lord! I didn't know you had
             company. Sorry, Lucy. (*To ANNA, not
             unpleasantly*) You should have told me,
             silly girl!

LUCY:        Come in, Barbara! (*To ANNA*) That's all
             right, Anna.

*ANNA goes out.*

BARBARA:     (*Nodding towards Anna*) Can't understand
             a blessed word she says … (*To CLIVE*)
             Hello, Clive! How are you?

CLIVE:       I'm all right, Barbara. (*Introducing
             LAURENCE and the INSPECTOR*) Mr
             Hudson – Inspector Kenton – Lady
             Barstow.

BARBARA:     Good evening, Inspector.

KENTON:      Good evening, Lady Barstow.

BARBARA:     (*To LAURENCE*) We've met before,
             haven't we?

*LAURENCE crosses and shakes hands.*

46

LAURENCE: Yes, I believe we have. Wasn't it at the Regatta?

BARBARA: Yes, of course! That wretched Regatta! (*Turns towards LUCY*) Well, I'm on the usual scrounge, Lucy.

LUCY: What is it this time?

BARBARA: You know that trolley of yours – the garden contraption – the one you serve drinks from?

LUCY: Yes.

BARBARA: D'you think I could borrow it for a couple of days?

LUCY: Yes, of course, Barbara.

BARBARA: I've got some people coming down for the weekend. (*To CLIVE*) Got to put on a bit of a show, you know. Frightful snobs. Haven't got a bob.

LUCY: What about the glasses?

BARBARA: Well – I was coming to that. If you could lend me half-a dozen. Those Swedish ones, Lucy – you know.

LUCY: (*Nodding*) Yes, I know.

BARBARA: I'll send Harper over tomorrow morning for the trolley. I'll collect the glasses myself at the weekend.

KENTON: Lady Barstow.

BARBARA: (*Turning*) Yes.

KENTON: I understand you had some photographs taken a little while ago by a man called Pelford?

BARBARA: Pelford?

KENTON: Profile, Ltd.

BARBARA: Oh, that's right! Yes, I did. Had the dogs taken. Very good, too. Excellent. (*To*

47

|  |  |
|---|---|
| | *LUCY*) I think I showed them to you, Lucy. |
| LUCY: | Yes, you did. |
| BARBARA: | (*To KENTON*) Oh, absolutely first class. Life-like … |
| KENTON: | How did you come of hear of this firm, Lady Barstow? |
| BARBARA: | Oh, Lord, now you've asked me something. I think I saw an advertisement in The Canine Weekly – or was it the Berkshire Herald? I'm not sure. |
| KENTON: | (*Smiling*) Anyway, you were very satisfied with them. |
| BARBARA: | Oh, absolutely. The man's first class. Flaps around a bit, mark you. The usual chi-chi nonsense. You know these photographers. |
| KENTON: | Where did he take the photographs – here, or in Town? |
| BARBARA: | Good heavens, here, of course! You don't think I took the dogs up to London! I'm not that stupid. |
| KENTON: | Lady Barstow, tell me – when Pelford was down here did he mention Mrs Freeman at all? |
| BARBARA: | (*Puzzled*) Mrs Freeman? |
| KENTON: | Yes … or Mr Freeman, of course, or Janet? |
| BARBARA: | No.  No, not that I recall. |
| KENTON: | Did he suggest that you recommend him to Mrs Freeman? |
| BARBARA: | No, I don't think so. |
| KENTON: | But you did. |
| BARBARA: | Did what? |

48

KENTON:      You did recommend him.

BARBARA:     (*A shade puzzled and irritated*) Yes, of
             course I did! He was damned good. I say, I
             may be dense – but what's the point of all
             this?

KENTON:      (*Pleasantly*) It's nothing – I was just a
             little curious, that's all.

*BARBARA looks at him for a moment, then turns towards
LUCY.*

BARBARA:     I'll send Harper over tomorrow morning.

LUCY:        Yes, all right, Barbara. I'll have the trolley
             ready for you.

BARBARA:     Er – did I say half-a-dozen glasses?

LUCY:        You did – but you can borrow the set, like
             you usually do.

BARBARA:     (*Pleased*) Oh, thanks. Thanks a lot. (*To
             CLIVE*) Goodnight, Clive.

CLIVE:       Goodnight, Barbara.

KENTON:      Goodnight, Lady Barstow.

BARBARA:     Goodnight.

*She moves towards the door, nods to LAURENCE and the
INSPECTOR and goes out.*

KENTON:      (*To LUCY, quietly*) Is this the photograph,
             Mrs Freeman?

LUCY:        Yes.

*KENTON takes the photograph and looks at it.*

KENTON:      Where's Janet?

*CLIVE crosses and points to a figure on the photograph.*

CLIVE:       There she is, but you'd never recognise
             her.

LAURENCE:    It's none of my business, Inspector, but
             why do you want that photograph if it's
             not a very good one?

49

KENTON:     I want Mrs Freeman to use it … (*He looks across at LUCY*) … As an excuse for calling on Mr Pelford …

CUT TO: *A taxi drives up to an arcade near Baker Street. LUCY gets out of the taxi, pays the driver and crosses the pavement. She stops for a moment and looks at a group of photographs in a showcase entrance to the arcade. The name "Profile LTD" is above the showcase and the case mainly contains photographs of animals and very young children. LUCY is carrying an envelope containing the school photograph. She passes into the arcade.*

CUT TO:   ROY PELFORD's Studio, Baker Street.
The studio is a large, untidy attic-style room, with several chairs, a dilapidated settee, numerous framed photographs, easels, cameras and photographic material.
*PELFORD is stood at an easel-style desk, examining a photograph. He is a thin, untidy, faintly bohemian-looking man in his early thirties. He wears glasses and has a rather detached air of superiority. There is a kettle boiling on a small gas ring, a teapot and cups are on a nearby tray. The door buzzer sounds and after a moment PELFORD puts down the negative and crosses to the door. When he opens it, LUCY is standing in the doorway.*
LUCY:       (*A shade nervous*) Mr Pelford?
PELFORD:    Yes.
LUCY:       I'm Mrs Freeman.
PELFORD:    (*After a moment; scrutinising her*) Oh, Mrs Freeman! How very nice of you to call. Do come in.
*LUCY enters the studio. PELFORD crosses and removes several articles from the settee.*

LUCY:          I don't know whether you remember me,
               Mr Pelford. We haven't actually met
               before, but …
PELFORD:       Of course I remember you. We spoke on
               the telephone, just before your little girl …
               (*He stops*)
LUCY:          Yes, that's right.
PELFORD:       (*Indicating the settee*) Do sit down. I'm
               afraid the room's a bit of a shambles at the
               moment. I'm in the process of sorting
               things out. (*A brief smile*) I nearly always
               am in the process of sorting things out,
               Mrs Freeman.

*LUCY sits down. PELFORD crosses to the gas ring.*

PELFORD:       Would you like a cup of tea?
LUCY:          No, thank you.

*PELFORD takes the kettle off the ring and pours the water
into the teapot on the tray. He stands looking at LUCY as
he mixes himself a cup of tea.*

LUCY:          (*Indicating the envelope*) I've brought this
               photograph along. I was wondering if you
               could enlarge it for me.
PELFORD:       What is it a photograph of?
LUCY:          My daughter.
PELFORD:       Let me see it.

*LUCY opens the envelope and takes out the photograph.
PELFORD puts down his cup of tea, crosses and takes the
photograph. He looks at it.*

LUCY:          (*After a moment*) It's a school photograph.
PELFORD:       So I see.
LUCY:          Is it possible to block the other children
               out and just enlarge Janet?

*PELFORD looks at her.*

PELFORD: It is possible, but it wouldn't be very satisfactory. (*Smiling*) And we do like to give satisfaction.

*There is a slight pause.*

*PELFORD puts down the photograph and turns and picks up his cup of tea. He crosses down to LUCY still holding the cup in his hand. He stands looking at her for a moment. LUCY is obviously ill at ease, faintly embarrassed.*

PELFORD: This is a most unfortunate business. I do sympathise.

*LUCY rises from the settee and faces PELFORD.*

LUCY: (*Tensely*) You know why I came here this afternoon?

PELFORD: Of course. (*Indicating the photograph*) There was no need to bring this. (*Smiles*) You didn't need an excuse, Mrs Freeman.

LUCY: We saw the name Profile in the exercise book.

PELFORD: (*Nodding*) Yes, I know. I told Mr Hudson you'd be interested in the exercise book.

LUCY: Who wrote those words? Who wrote the words – Pictures – Photographs – Profile?

PELFORD: (*Faintly surprised*) Why, your daughter did – didn't you recognise the handwriting?

LUCY: When did she write them?

PELFORD: Two days ago.

LUCY: (*Tensely and angry*) Where is Janet? What have you done with her?

PELFORD: Mrs Freeman, do sit down. I find it a little disconcerting facing an angry mother with a cup of tea in my hand.

52

| | |
|---|---|
| LUCY: | (*Quietly, controlling herself*) Where is Janet? |
| PELFORD: | (*A moment's hesitation, then*) She's staying with some friends of mine. She's in very good health and extremely well taken care of. |
| LUCY: | Mr Pelford, if you don't tell me where Janet is, I shall send for the police! – Now! Immediately! |

*There is a pause.*

| | |
|---|---|
| PELFORD: | (*Quietly*) That would be a very stupid thing to do. |

*A moment.*

| | |
|---|---|
| LUCY: | (*Facing him, quietly*) What is it you want? If it's a question of money … |
| PELFORD: | Unfortunately, it isn't. My friends and I disagree on that point, but – (*A shrug*) they insist, it isn't a question of money. |
| LUCY: | Well – what do you want? |
| PELFORD: | From you? Co-operation. |
| LUCY: | Co-operation? |

*PELFORD looks at LUCY, then quietly finishes his cup of tea and puts down the cup.*

| | |
|---|---|
| PELFORD: | How many people know about this afternoon? |
| LUCY: | No one knows. |
| PELFORD: | No one? |
| LUCY: | My husband, of course, but – no one else. |
| PELFORD: | Didn't you tell Inspector Kenton you were coming to see me? |
| LUCY: | (*Tensely, faintly angry*) I've told you. No one knows I'm here. No one knows I'm here except my husband! |

PELFORD:     Mrs Freeman, you and I have got to get on
             well together. We've got to see eye to eye.
             We've got to co-operate. If we don't,
             things might get out of hand. Now we
             don't want that to happen, do we?

LUCY:        (*Angrily*) Look, I've asked you what it is
             you want …

PELFORD:     And I've told you. Co-operation. The
             truth.

LUCY:        I've told you the truth.

*PELFORD slowly shakes his head.*

PELFORD:     Inspector Kenton knows you're here – so
             does Superintendent Wilde. You've
             arranged to meet Kenton this afternoon at
             a teashop in Leicester Square.

LUCY:        (*Not very convincing*) That's not true.

PELFORD:     (*Quietly, pleasantly*) It is. You know it is.
             Now don't let's be stupid about this.

*LUCY rises, almost defeated.*

LUCY:        What is it you want me to do?

*There is a pause.*

*PELFORD still looks at LUCY. He looks pleased with
himself. His next remark takes her completely by surprise.*

PELFORD:     Would you like to speak to Janet?

LUCY:        (*Amazed*) Is Janet here? Is she …

PELFORD:     (*Interrupting her*) No, no, no! But since
             we're going to be friends, Mrs Freeman –
             and I'm sure we are going to be friends – I
             thought perhaps you might like to speak to
             your daughter; just to reassure yourself
             that she's perfectly all right.

*PELFORD crosses to the telephone, picks it up, turns his
back on LUCY and dials a number; when he has finished
dialling he turns round and faces her again. We hear the*

54

*ringing tone. LUCY slowly crosses towards him. The receiver is lifted at the other end.*

LOMAX:      (*On the other end*) Hello?

PELFORD:    Mrs Freeman's here. Bring the little girl to the phone.

*PELFORD hands LUCY the receiver. She stands tense, waiting.*

CUT TO:   A small room.

*LOMAX is standing by a radiogram turntable; a similar turntable to those used in broadcasting studios. LOMAX holds the telephone receiver in his left hand and the head of the tone arm in his right. LOMAX is a dark, swarthy-looking man. He wears horn-rimmed glasses and a bow tie. The turntable is revolving and he is about to place the tone arm on a record.*

LUCY:    (*On the other end of the line*) Hello?

*As soon as LOMAX hears LUCY's voice he puts the tone arm on the record and moves the telephone receiver nearer to the instrument.*

CUT TO:   ROY PELFORD's studio. As before.

*LUCY is holding the receiver.*

LUCY:    Hello?

JANET'S VOICE: (*From the other end*) Hello, Mummy … This is Janet … How are you, Mummy?

LUCY:    (*Tensely*) Janet, are you all right? Darling, where are you? Where are you speaking from …?

JANET'S VOICE: There's nothing to worry about … I'm perfectly all right … Honestly, Mummy … Give Daddy my love ...

*LOMAX replaces the receiver at the other end and the dialling tone starts.*

LUCY:       Darling, now listen to me! I want you to …
            (*Realising the receiver has been replaced*)
            Janet! Janet … (*She looks at the receiver in
            her hand*)

*PELFORD quietly takes the receiver out of her hand and
replaces it.*

PELFORD: (*Quietly; almost with consideration*) Sit
            down, Mrs Freeman.

*LUCY stares at him, tense, confused, her thoughts
elsewhere. After a moment she sits down on the settee.*

*There is a pause.*

PELFORD: (*Looking down at LUCY*) Well, you know
            she's all right, anyway. And she's going to be
            all right. I'm sure there's no need for you to
            worry – if you listen to what I've got to say.

*LUCY looks up at PELFORD. After a moment he
continues.*

PELFORD: There are two things you can do about this
            afternoon. You can tell Inspector Kenton
            exactly what's happened; you can tell him
            what I've said to you, you can tell him about
            the telephone call. Or alternatively …

LUCY:       Yes?

PELFORD: Or alternatively, you can be sensible, Mrs
            Freeman.


CUT TO:  A CAFÉ

*DETECTIVE INSPECTOR KENTON and CLIVE are
sitting at a small table in a Leicester Square café.
KENTON's pipe is on an ashtray.*

CLIVE:      … She's been gone well over an hour.

KENTON: (*Quietly*) Yes, I know. But Pelford might
            have been out – he might have been busy,

56

perhaps he kept her waiting. I don't think there's any cause for alarm, Mr Freeman.

CLIVE: (*Irritated*) I'm not alarmed. I'm just a little anxious, that's all.

*KENTON puts down his cup and picks up his pipe.*

KENTON: I told Superintendent Wilde about the puppet.

CLIVE: What did he say?

KENTON: He was interested.

CLIVE: Was it a coincidence?

KENTON: The name?

CLIVE: Yes.

KENTON: I don't know. Apparently, there is a Mr Nelson and Wilde's particularly interested in him. On the other hand, one must admit that was a pretty obvious name for the puppet.

CLIVE: When you say there is a Mr Nelson and Wilde's interested in him do you mean …

KENTON: (*Interrupting him*) I mean just that, Mr Freeman. Nothing more. Wilde's a Scotland Yard man and they're notoriously uncommunicative when it comes to … (*He breaks off and rises from the table*)

*CLIVE turns his head and also gets up as LUCY arrives.*

CLIVE: Did you see him?

LUCY: (*Tensely*) Yes.

KENTON: Sit down, Mrs Freeman.

*KENTON offers LUCY his chair and draws up another one from a nearby table. LUCY sits down.*

CLIVE: Well – what happened?

*There is a pause.*

KENTON: (*Looking at her, quietly*) Would you like a cup of tea?

LUCY: (*Hesitant, nervous*) Yes, I think I would, thank you, Inspector.

57

*KENTON looks up and nods to a waitress.*

CLIVE:    (*Anxiously*) Lucy, what happened? Did you ask him about …

LUCY:     (*Suddenly, controlling herself*) Nothing happened. (*To KENTON*) I did exactly what you told me to do. I showed him the photograph that I wanted an enlargement … He was quite nice about it. He said he could do it but it wouldn't be very satisfactory … After that we talked about Janet … He'd read all about it of course … He was really quite nice … most sympathetic.

KENTON: Go on, Mrs Freeman …

LUCY:     I told him about the exercise book, about the name Profile … He was quite genuinely amazed – bewildered, in fact. He asked me if he ought to get in touch with the police about it, and I said … (*Hesitates*)

KENTON: And what did you say?

LUCY:     I said it wasn't necessary – you already knew about it.

KENTON: I see.

*A moment.*

CLIVE:    How did he strike you, Lucy? What's he like?

LUCY:     Oh, he's not very easy to describe. He's a curious type of man, I suppose, but – quite kind.

*CLIVE nods and looks across at KENTON who is sucking his pipe.*

*A pause.*

CLIVE:    Well, Inspector – where do we go from here?

*KENTON continues to look at Lucy, still sucking his pipe. After a moment he removes it from his mouth.*

KENTON:     (*With almost a touch of sympathy*) Would
            you like some cake, Mrs Freeman – or just
            a cup of tea?
LUCY:       (*Faintly surprised by the question*) Just a
            cup of tea, thank you.

*KENTON smiles and nods.*

CUT TO:  The Drawing Room at Amberley. Three hours
later.

*LAURENCE HUDSON is sitting in an armchair reading a
glossy magazine. He is a shade restless. We hear the
sound of a car drawing up on the drive outside.
LAURENCE rises and crosses to the French windows.
After a moment he returns and moves towards the main
door leading to the hall. CLIVE enters, taking off his hat
and overcoat as he does so. He is followed by ANNA, who
takes the hat and coat and returns to the hall.*

CLIVE:      (*Obviously tired*) Sorry to have kept you
            waiting, Laurence. It's taken us nearly two
            hours from Town. The traffic was
            appalling. (*He crosses to  the drinks table
            and begins to mix himself a whiskey and
            soda*) My God, I could use a drink.

*A moment.*

LAURENCE:  Where's Lucy?
CLIVE:      She'll be down in a minute.
LAURENCE:  Did she see Profile?

*CLIVE moves to LAURENCE, holding the drink in his
hand.*

CLIVE:      Pelford, you mean? Yes, she saw him but
            – (*Suddenly realising he hasn't offered
            LAURENCE a drink*) Oh, I beg your
            pardon, Laurence! What would you like?

59

LAURENCE: No, no, nothing for me, Clive. (*Intensely curious*) Tell me what happened? What did he say?

CLIVE: (*After a drink*) Nothing happened. He said he knew nothing about Janet – about the exercise book … He couldn't account for the name being in it …

LAURENCE: But didn't Lucy tell him …

CLIVE: (*Interrupting, a shade 'on edge'*) I don't know what Lucy told him, all I know is Pelford said he knew nothing about it.

LAURENCE: (*A moment, then:*) I don't believe it. I think he's lying. It's far too big a coincidence for my liking.

*LUCY enters from the hall.*

CLIVE: Well, that's what I think. But Lucy seems completely … (*He breaks off*)

LUCY: Lucy seems completely what?

CLIVE: (*Irritated: dismissing the matter*) We were talking about Pelford – about this afternoon.

LAURENCE: Hello, Lucy!

LUCY: I'm sorry we kept you waiting, Laurence. It took us ages to get out of Town.

LAURENCE: Yes, so Clive told me.

LUCY: I've never seen such traffic.

CLIVE: (*Softly, to LUCY*) I expect you could do with a drink, Lucy. What would you like?

*LUCY looks at him, surprised by the warmth of his voice.*

LUCY: (*With a suggestion of emotion*) I think I'd like a whiskey and soda.

*CLIVE nods and looks across at LAURENCE who shakes his head. CLIVE crosses to the drinking table and proceeds to mix the drink. LAURENCE looks at LUCY,*

*aware of her nearness to tears. He crosses, takes out his
cigarette case and offers her a cigarette. She moves to take
one then, with a shake of her head, changes her mind and
moves across to the settee. CLIVE returns with the drink.*

CLIVE:         (*Handing LUCY the glass*) I've forgotten
               the soda – so be careful.

*LUCY nods and drinks. CLIVE returns to the table to
replenish his own drink.*

LAURENCE:  Lucy, I asked Clive about this afternoon.
               About what happened between you and
               Pelford.

LUCY:          (*Quietly*) Clive doesn't know what
               happened …

*LAURENCE is surprised. He looks at LUCY, then across
at CLIVE. CLIVE leaves the drinks table and comes
towards LUCY.*

CLIVE:         (*To LUCY*) What do you mean, Lucy, I
               don't know? I thought you told Kenton
               and I … (*He stops and stares at LUCY*)
               Didn't you tell us the truth this afternoon?

*LUCY shakes her head and rises from the settee.*

LUCY:          No.

CLIVE:         (*Quickly; taking hold of LUCY's shoulder*)
               Then what did happen? (*Tensely*) What
               happened this afternoon?

LAURENCE:  Clive, please! (*To LUCY*) Why didn't you
               tell Clive the truth?

*LUCY hesitates. She is obviously under an emotional
strain.*

LUCY:          I daren't … I didn't want the Inspector to
               know anything about it. I promised Pelford
               that …

CLIVE:         (*Tensely*) Lucy, what happened?

| LUCY: | We were right about the exercise book … About the name … It was put there deliberately for our benefit … |
| CLIVE: | Go on … |
| LUCY: | Pelford knew about Janet … He's mixed up in this business, I don't know how, but … |
| CLIVE: | Lucy, what happened? What did he say? |
| LUCY: | (*A moment, looking up at CLIVE*) Someone's … going to get in touch with you … |
| CLIVE: | When? |
| LUCY: | Before the end of the week. If you do exactly what they say … Janet … will be all right. |
| CLIVE: | (*Angry*) Who told you that – Pelford? |
| LUCY: | Yes. |
| CLIVE: | Why, you fool, Lucy! Don't you realise you can't trust … |
| LAURENCE: | (*Stopping him*) Clive, wait a minute! Go on, Lucy – what else did he say? |
| LUCY: | He said I could go to the police and tell them the whole story if I wanted to … but if I did … we'd probably never see Janet again … |
| CLIVE: | (*Quietly*) You should have told Kenton the truth. He would have arrested the swine and by now … |
| LUCY: | (*Turning on him*) And where would that get us if Pelford contradicted my story, or refused to talk? Janet's been gone almost a fortnight and the police have discovered precisely nothing! I tell you, Clive, this is |

|  | our only chance! If we don't take it … (*She is near to tears*) |
|---|---|
| CLIVE: | (*Stopping her, quietly*) Lucy, wait a minute! Hasn't it occurred to you that there may be a reason why the police haven't discovered anything? |
| LUCY: | Yes, it's occurred to me, Clive, on more than one occasion. (*Shaking her head*) But it's not too late, if that's what you're thinking. |
| LAURENCE: | What do you mean, Lucy? |
| LUCY: | I spoke to Janet this afternoon, on the telephone – she's perfectly all right … |
| CLIVE: | (*Stunned*) My God! Lucy … Are you sure it was Janet? |
| LUCY: | Yes … Yes, it was Janet. |
| LAURENCE: | What happened? |
| LUCY: | Pelford telephoned someone … Janet came to the phone. (*Trying to control herself*) She's all right, Clive … she sounded – quite … quite all right … |

*CLIVE is obviously deeply moved. He stands looking at LUCY for a moment before he speaks.*

| CLIVE: | Lucy, what do you want me to do? |
|---|---|
| LUCY: | (*Looking up*) Don't go to the police … Wait and see what happens … Please, Clive, if it's only for forty-eight hours … Wait … |

*CLIVE looks worried, desperately concerned. After a moment he takes LUCY by the shoulder and quietly nods his head. LAURENCE stands watching them.*

CUT TO:   The Drawing Room. Two days later.

*BARBARA is examining one of the ornaments on a pedestal table. She hears someone coming, hastily replaces the ornament and returns to the settee. CLIVE enters from the sun lounge.*

CLIVE:         Hello, Barbara! I'm sorry Lucy's out at the moment. I think she's gone down into the village.

BARBARA:   (*Disappointed*) Oh, Lord! (*Rises*) Well, I'll give her a tinkle tomorrow morning.

CLIVE:         Is there anything I can do?

BARBARA:   Well – it's about that trolley, Clive. The one we borrowed for the weekend.

CLIVE:         Yes.

BARBARA:   We had a sort of dress rehearsal this morning. You know, opened it up – squatted ourselves in the jolly old deck chairs.

CLIVE:         Well?

BARBARA:   Well, it didn't look right somehow. I don't know what it is. We all looked so short-arsed.

CLIVE:         (*Smiling*) It's the chairs, Barbara. We had ours specially made when we bought the trolley.

BARBARA:   Ah, that's it! That's exactly what I said to Edward.

CLIVE:         And what did Edward say?

BARBARA:   (*Laughing*) Well, if you must know, he said …

CLIVE:         (*Interrupting*) Why the hell didn't you borrow the chairs while you were at it!

BARBARA:   (*A little laugh, but slightly taken aback*) Er – yes …

CLIVE: You can borrow three of them, Barbara, but we must have them back by Monday.

BARBARA: Yes, of course. Thanks, Clive. Thanks a lot.

CLIVE: Now, if you'll excuse me …

BARBARA: Yes, rather! Sorry to have barged in like this. (*Suddenly*) Oh, just a minute, there was something else … Now what the devil was it? (*A moment*) Oh, I remember – photographs! You remember the other day that detective chap asked me who recommended Pelford or Profile Ltd., or whatever he calls himself?

CLIVE: Yes – you said you'd seen an advertisement.

BARBARA: Well, I didn't. I've remembered since. I heard about Pelford from Robert Stevens. We were talking about photographs one day and he said …

CLIVE: Who's Robert Stevens?

BARBARA: He's my dentist. (*Faintly surprised*) Don't you go to him? South Bank Chambers … He's awfully good.

CLIVE: No, I've got a man in Town – but go on, Barbara.

BARBARA: Well, we were talking about photographs and Stevens mentioned Pelford – gave him a terrific build-up, said he was frightfully good with animals.

CLIVE: Are you sure it was Stevens who recommended him?

BARBARA: Why, yes. (*A sudden thought*) Unless, of course, it was that accountant chap – Harcourt. Now, was it Harcourt? No …

no, I'm pretty sure it was Stevens. (*Obviously not at all sure*) Yes, I'm pretty sure …

CLIVE: (*Not convinced*) Yes, all right, Barbara. (*He walks with her towards the door*) I'll have the chairs ready tomorrow morning. Tell Harper to bring the brake.

*They go out into the hall.*

BARBARA: (*Off, fading away*) Well, our brake's a bit temperamental at the moment, Clive. If we could borrow yours for an hour or two …

*LUCY enters from the sun lounge. She stands looking towards the hall. After a moment CLIVE returns.*

CLIVE: Did you hear all that?

LUCY: Yes, but she's impossible, you just can't rely on anything she says.

CLIVE: Had you heard of Stevens before?

LUCY: Yes. I went to him about a year ago. Don't you remember? I had howling toothache one night and …

CLIVE: Yes, of course! He's a young chap, frightfully good looking.

LUCY: That's right. He's only been down here about two years, but apparently all the women …

*The telephone starts to ring. CLIVE and LUCY look across at it. It continues to ring. CLIVE slowly crosses the room and after a moment picks up the receiver.*

CLIVE: Hello?

PELFORD: (*On the other end*) Is that Beacherscross 189?

CLIVE: Yes.

PELFORD: Mr Freeman?

CLIVE: Yes.

PELFORD:    Good evening, Mr Freeman. I think you've been expecting this call.

CLIVE:      Is that ... Pelford?

*LUCY moves and stands by CLIVE's side.*

PELFORD:    Yes, it is. Now, I haven't a lot of time, Mr Freeman, so I'll come straight to the point. Can you arrange to see a friend of mine tomorrow night?

CLIVE:      Yes.

PELFORD:    Splendid! Now this is what I want you to do. Arrange for your staff and Mrs Freeman to be out of the house by eight o'clock – half past eight at the latest.

CLIVE:      What do you mean – out of the house?

PELFORD:    I mean – out of the house. When my friend calls there must be no one in the house. No one – except yourself. Is that quite clear?

CLIVE:      Yes.

PELFORD:    I hope it is, Mr Freeman.

CLIVE:      (*Quickly*) Yes. Yes, it's quite clear. I understand.

PELFORD:    Very well. Goodnight.

CLIVE:      No, wait – wait a minute. What do they call this friend of yours?

PELFORD:    The name is unimportant. He'll be there at nine o'clock. Goodnight. (*He replaces the receiver*)

*CLIVE looks at LUCY.*

CUT TO:   The drawing room the following night.

The curtains are drawn across the French windows. The room is deserted, the only light coming from a side table and a standard lamp.

*There is the sound of someone tapping a small metallic object (probably a coin) against the French windows. This tapping continues for a moment or two then stops. CLIVE enters from the hall. His manner is quick and faintly tense. He looks at his watch, crosses to the writing desk and as he does so the tapping noise starts again, and he quickly turns and looks towards the French windows. The tapping continues. CLIVE crosses the room, turns out all the lights and then moves over to the French windows. He draws back the curtains and opens the window. A man enters the room. CLIVE closes the window, draws the curtains, then turns and switches on all the lights. The man is revealed as LAURENCE. He is wearing a light overcoat and looks distinctly tired.*

CLIVE: (*A shade annoyed*) I thought you weren't coming, Laurence.

LAURENCE: I had a puncture and had to walk part of the way.

CLIVE: Good heavens, tonight of all nights!

LAURENCE: I'd like a drink, Clive.

CLIVE: Yes, of course. (*Crosses to the drink table*) Where did you leave the car?

LAURENCE: Outside of the pub in Kingsdown. I didn't know what to do with it. I knew I was late, but I didn't want to waste time telephoning.

CLIVE: Which way did you come?

LAURENCE: The way you said. Round Thompson's Paddock and across the fields.

CLIVE: Did you see anyone?

LAURENCE: No. (*Taking a drink from CLIVE*) Thanks.

*LAURENCE drinks. CLIVE glances at his watch again.*

LAURENCE: Lucy's out, I take it?

CLIVE: Yes, she went out this afternoon. I made her go up to Town.

LAURENCE: And Anna?

CLIVE: She's gone over to some friends in Beaconsfield. She's staying the night.

LAURENCE: (*Obviously a shade nervous: apprehensive*) Clive, I'm worried about this. I think you're making a mistake.

CLIVE: You mean I should have gone to Kenton and told him the whole story?

LAURENCE: No. No, that's not what I mean. (*Hesitant*) I think that's what you should have done in the first place. But …

CLIVE: (*A shade impatiently*) Well, what do you mean, Laurence?

LAURENCE: You shouldn't have phoned me, Clive. You shouldn't have told me anything about this.

CLIVE: (*Nodding*) I wasn't going to, but Lucy insisted. I think she thought – anyway, you're here now, and there's nothing we can do about it.

*The doorbell rings.*

LAURENCE: It seems such an unnecessary risk. If they find out there's someone here besides yourself, they'll think you've double-crossed them, and the chances are … (*He stops speaking, obviously having heard the doorbell*)

CLIVE: That's the doorbell. Pelford said nine o'clock.

LAURENCE: (*Nervously, yet with a note of efficiency*) Now what do you want me to do?

*CLIVE indicates the sun lounge door.*

CLIVE: Wait in the sun lounge. Stay there until you hear from me. I'll let you know the moment he's gone.

*LAURENCE nods, puts down his glass, and goes out through the sun lounge door. CLIVE looks round the room, picks up LAURENCE's glass, returns it to the drinks table, then he goes out into the hall. After a moment we hear the sound of the front door being opened. LAURENCE comes out of the sun lounge, looks round the drawing room, sees his glass on the drinks table, crosses, picks it up, then quickly returns to the sun lounge. There is the sound of voices in the hall.*

CLIVE: (*Off*) You'd better go into the drawing room. It's on the left.

*The VISITOR enters the room, followed by CLIVE. The VISITOR is a serious-looking man of about forty. He wears a dark grey overcoat, a grey hat, and carries a walking stick. He takes off the hat as he enters the room. His manner is quiet and completely impersonal. He looks round the room, crosses to the window, glances behind the curtains and then returns to CLIVE who is standing near the settee, watching him.*

VISITOR: Are we alone?

CLIVE: Yes.

VISITOR: There's no-one else in the house?

CLIVE: (*Shaking his head*) No-one.

VISITOR: Where's your wife?

CLIVE: She's in London. She went out this afternoon. She won't be back until late this evening.

*THE VISITOR points to the door leading to the sun lounge.*

VISITOR: Where does that lead to?

70

CLIVE:    It's a sun lounge. There's no one in there. (*A shrug*) You can look if you like.

*The VISITOR ignores the invitation and moves down to CLIVE. He puts his stick down on the back of the settee. CLIVE sits on the arm of the settee.*

VISITOR: Mr Freeman, I'm sure you'd prefer it if I came straight to the point. You have something we want. We have …

CLIVE:    (*Interrupting him*) We? Who's we?

VISITOR: (*Quietly*) Myself – and certain other people. However, there's no need for you to get involved with personalities. The issue so far as you are concerned is really quite simple.

CLIVE:    I'm all for simplicity.

VISITOR: Very well. If you do what I want you to do, tomorrow afternoon your daughter will be taken into Regent's Park and handed over to Mrs Freeman. She's in very good health and I assure you none the worse for her experience.

CLIVE:    And supposing I don't do what you want me to do?

VISITOR: (*Quite simply*) Then your daughter will not be taken into Regent's Park, and she will not be handed over to Mrs Freeman.

CLIVE:    What is it you want? If it's a question of money …

VISITOR: (*The first suggestion of irritation*) It is not a question of money. I thought Pelford had made that quite clear.

CLIVE:    Then what is it?

VISITOR: You have certain information, Mr Freeman. Rightly or wrongly, my friends and I consider that information of some importance.

71

CLIVE: Are you sure you know what you're talking about?

*There is a noise from the sun lounge. CLIVE realises this but ignores it.*

CLIVE: I'm a businessman. What possible information could I have that would be worth …

VISITOR: Wait!

*The VISITOR turns and moves across to the sun lounge. He takes a revolver out of his coat pocket. CLIVE rises and moves towards him.*

CLIVE: (*Tensely*) What is it?

VISITOR: (*Turning, looking at him*) You said the house was empty.

CLIVE: It is …

VISITOR: (*Shaking his head: indicating the door*) I don't think so. There's someone in there.

CLIVE: I can assure you …

VISITOR: (*With authority*) There's someone in there! Tell them to come out!

*A moment.*

CLIVE: (*Quietly*) Very well.

*The VISITOR turns towards the door leading into the sun lounge. He raises the revolver, pointing it towards the door.*

CLIVE: (*Nervously, raising his voice*) Come out, Laurence!

*The VISITOR ignores Clive. Suddenly CLIVE picks up the walking stick off the back of the settee and springs forward toward the man. The VISITOR senses what is happening, and instinctively turns. The stick cracks down on his head and then falls to the floor. The VISITOR reels under the impact of the blow and CLIVE immediately takes advantage of this and tries to get possession of the revolver. LAURENCE rushes out of the sun lounge. There*

*is a revolver shot and the VISITOR falls to the ground. CLIVE stares at the VISITOR in amazement, breathless and confused. LAURENCE looks across at CLIVE, apparently bewildered. After a moment he moves forward and kneels down by the body. CLIVE stands transfixed, watching LAURENCE as he briefly examines the VISITOR. After a moment LAURENCE looks up.*
LAURENCE: (*Looking at CLIVE*) He's dead …

# END OF EPISODE TWO

# EPISODE THREE

OPEN TO: The Drawing room at Amberley.

*LAURENCE HUDSON is kneeling by the body of the VISITOR with CLIVE standing in the background.*

CLIVE:         … Are you sure he's dead, Laurence?

LAURENCE:   (*Quietly; nodding*) Yes.

CLIVE:         My God, what are we going to do?

LAURENCE:   There's only one thing you can do. You'll have to phone the police and tell them exactly what happened.

CLIVE:         But – do you think they'll believe me?

LAURENCE:   Yes, I think so. They're bound to believe you. Only … (*Changes his mind*)

CLIVE:         Only what?

*LAURENCE shakes his head, like Clive he is tense and undecided.*

LAURENCE:   Nothing. It doesn't matter.

*LAURENCE crosses to the open door of the sun lounge and picks up a pair of spectacles which are on the floor.*

LAURENCE:   (*Returning to CLIVE with spectacles*) These damn things fell out of my pocket while I was trying to listen to what was going on …

CLIVE:         (*Tensely*) Laurence, what were you going to say just now?

LAURENCE:   (*Shaking his head*) Nothing. Nothing, Clive.

CLIVE:         Laurence, what is it?

LAURENCE:   Well – (*Looks down at the body*) I was just thinking. If you tell the police, the people who sent him here are bound to find out what happened … They'll think you deliberately double-crossed them, and then the chances of getting Janet …

CLIVE: (*Interrupting him, with an emphatic nod*) I know … that's what I was thinking.

LAURENCE: Still, you'll have to tell the police, there's nothing else you can do.

CLIVE: Laurence, wait a minute! Supposing I make out I've never seen him.

LAURENCE: What do you mean?

CLIVE: Supposing I phone Pelford tomorrow morning – or late tonight for that matter – and tell him no one turned up?

LAURENCE: You wouldn't get away with it. They know he came here.

CLIVE: How do you know they know? Perhaps he never arrived. Perhaps something happened to him before he got here.

*LAURENCE shakes his head.*

CLIVE: Well, supposing I swear I've never seen him! Supposing I lose my temper with Pelford and accuse them of trying to double-cross me?

LAURENCE: You might get away with it, I suppose. (*Thoughtfully*) I don't know. How did he get here – by car?

CLIVE: No. He must have come by train and walked up from the station.

*LAURENCE looks down at the body.*

LAURENCE: Who is he, Clive? What's his name?

CLIVE: I don't know.

*LAURENCE looks at CLIVE for a moment, then kneels down and begins to search the man's pockets. They are empty except for the inside pocket of the jacket from which LAURENCE produces a wallet. He opens it and as he does so, a piece of paper falls to the ground. CLIVE immediately picks it up and looks at it.*

78

CLIVE:        (*Suddenly, looking at the piece of paper*)
              Laurence, his name's Nelson …
LAURENCE:     (*Looking up from the wallet*) Nelson?
              Then this must be the man Wilde
              mentioned …
CLIVE:        It looks like it.

*He looks at the piece of paper again.*

LAURENCE:     What is it?
CLIVE:        It's a receipt. (*Reading from the paper*)
              South Bank Chambers … K. Nelson
              Esquire … To Mr Robert C. Stevens for
              professional services … Seven guineas.
LAURENCE:     Robert C. Stevens?
CLIVE:        He's a dentist in Kingsdown. Lady
              Barstow  mentioned him. She said it was
              Stevens that first told her about Pelford.

*LAURENCE takes the receipt from CLIVE and looks at it.*

LAURENCE:     (*After a moment*) It's a pity Nelson's
              address isn't on this.
CLIVE:        Perhaps it's in the wallet.

*LAURENCE turns and crosses to the desk. He empties the
contents of the wallet out onto it. The wallet contains
twelve English pound notes, two Swiss notes for a hundred
francs each and a cheque book.*

LAURENCE:     (*Examining the wallet*) There's nothing
              else … *He puts the notes back into the
              wallet, crosses to NELSON and returns the
              wallet to his inside pocket.*
CLIVE:        (*Watching him, quietly*) Laurence, I've
              made up my mind … I know what I'm
              going to do.
LAURENCE:     (*Straightening up; serious*) What?
CLIVE:        I want you to leave. I want you to go back
              to  Town – now – immediately.

LAURENCE: But that's absurd! I'm your only witness. Once the police start asking questions …

CLIVE: (*Interrupting*) The police aren't going to ask questions.

LAURENCE: What do you mean?

CLIVE: (*Nodding towards Nelson*) I'm taking him down to Henshaw Wood …

LAURENCE: (*Quietly, surprised*) Clive, you can't do that …

CLIVE: (*Tensely*) I've got to. You were right about this, Laurence – the more I think about it the more I realise it. I've got to convince Pelford that Nelson didn't come here.

LAURENCE: (*Quietly, looking at NELSON*) How are you going to get him to Henshaw – in your car?

CLIVE: Yes. It'll only take half-an-hour at this time of night.

*A pause.*

*LAURENCE stands deep in thought, obviously worried.*

LAURENCE: I don't like it, Clive. Apart from anything else, it's a terrible risk.

CLIVE: Look, Laurence – supposing you were in my shoes? Supposing Janet was your daughter …?

LAURENCE: I'd go to the police. I'd tell them the whole story …

CLIVE: (*Facing him*) Would you? Would you, Laurence?

*A pause.*

LAURENCE: And what about Lucy? What are you going to tell Lucy?

CLIVE:          (*Quite definite*) So far as Lucy's
                concerned, so far as anyone's concerned –
                he just didn't turn up.

*There is another pause, then LAURENCE suddenly makes
a decision.*

LAURENCE:   All right, Clive.  Have you got a rug – a
                large rug?

CLIVE:          Yes.

LAURENCE:   Where?

CLIVE:          In the sun lounge.

LAURENCE:   (*With quiet authority*) Right! You get the
                car. (*Nods towards Nelson*) I'll see to this.

*LAURENCE turns and goes to the sun lounge. CLIVE
stands for a moment looking after him, then he quickly
turns and goes out into the hall.*

CUT TO:  CLIVE's Bentley is parked on the top of a
small bank looking down into a thickly wooded copse
which is part of Henshaw Wood. The car is empty.
*We see CLIVE and LAURENCE emerging from the wood
and walking up the bank towards the car. CLIVE is
carrying the rug. The camera follows CLIVE and
LAURENCE up the bank and then slowly pans away to the
left and down into the undergrowth. We see the body of
NELSON concealed in one of the bushes, his hat and stick
have been placed by the body. We hear the sound of
CLIVE's car starting and being driven away.*

CUT TO:   The Drawing Room at Amberley.
The curtains are drawn, and the lights are on.
*CLIVE is standing by the desk, on the telephone.
LAURENCE, drink in hand, stands watching him.*

CLIVE: (*To LAURENCE*) … There doesn't seem to be any reply.

LAURENCE: Is it ringing?

CLIVE: Yes, it's been ringing for the last two or three minutes.

LAURENCE: Maybe he doesn't live at the studio. Perhaps he only works there.

CLIVE: That wasn't the impression I got from Lucy.

*In the background the front doorbell is ringing.*

LAURENCE: I think I'd leave it, Clive, and try tomorrow morning.

CLIVE: (*Thoughtfully*) I don't know. It seems to me that the sooner I get hold of him the better … (*Stops speaking, looks at LAURENCE*) That's the doorbell …

LAURENCE: Is it Lucy?

CLIVE: No, she's got her key.

*The doorbell continues to ring.*

LAURENCE: (*After a moment*) I'll answer it.

*CLIVE nods and LAURENCE goes out into the hall. CLIVE still holds the telephone receiver but stands, looks with curiosity towards the hall. After a moment there is the sound of voices. CLIVE replaces the receiver and walks towards the door, as LAURENCE returns with DETECTIVE INSPECTOR KENTON.*

LAURENCE: It's the Inspector, Clive.

CLIVE: (*A shade surprised, somewhat nervous*) Oh – come in, Inspector.

KENTON: Sorry to disturb you at this time of night, Mr Freeman.

CLIVE: That's all right. Is there any news?

KENTON: No, I'm afraid not, sir – but I was passing and I saw the light and I thought …

CLIVE:       Yes, yes, of course.  Would you like a drink?

KENTON:      Well, that's very kind of you, sir …

*LAURENCE crosses to the drinks table.*

LAURENCE:    What would you like?

KENTON:      (*To CLIVE*) May I have a whiskey and soda?

CLIVE:       Yes, certainly.

*LAURENCE mixes the drink.*

KENTON:      Mrs Freeman away for the weekend, sir?

CLIVE:       (*Curious*) No?

KENTON:      I saw her at the station this afternoon and I wondered if …

CLIVE:       (*A shade too casual*) No, no, she's just in town for the day, that's all. I think she's gone to a concert, this evening, I'm not sure.

*LAURENCE brings the drink over to the INSPECTOR.*

KENTON:      (*Taking the drink*) Thank you.

*KENTON raises his glass to CLIVE and LAURENCE and then drinks. CLIVE and LAURENCE look at him and are obviously curious about his visit. KENTON realises this and sits on the arm of the settee sipping his drink, taking his time.*

KENTON:      (*To CLIVE*) Well – I'll tell you why I dropped in, sir. I've been making further enquiries about that photographer chap – Pelford.

CLIVE:       Yes?

KENTON:      Now don't misunderstand me, sir. Naturally I accept Mrs Freeman's version of what happened the other afternoon, but nevertheless we've got to …

LAURENCE:    Pursue every avenue …

KENTON:     Exactly, sir.

CLIVE:      Go on, Inspector.

KENTON:     Well, I've made rather an interesting discovery. Whether it has any bearing on the case or not remains to be seen. I've discovered that Pelford has a sister …

CLIVE:      Well?

KENTON:     Do you know who she's married to, sir?

CLIVE:      No.

KENTON:     Dr Bramwell-Cane.

CLIVE:      (*Surprised*) Bramwell-Cane?

LAURENCE:   That name's familiar. (*To KENTON and CLIVE*) Where've I heard that before?

KENTON:     You remember Bramwell-Cane – the scientist. He worked at Prescott. Two years ago, he and his wife disappeared.

LAURENCE:   Good Lord, yes, of course! They're in Prague – they gave a newspaper interview about five or six weeks ago.

KENTON:     That's right, sir.

LAURENCE:   Well, forgive me, but what has this got to do with Mr Freeman – with the disappearance of his daughter?

KENTON:     I didn't say it's got anything to do with it, sir. It just struck me as being a rather odd coincidence.

CLIVE:      Why? Because I worked at Prescott?

KENTON:     Yes, sir.

CLIVE:      But I hardly knew Bramwell-Cane. I only met him about two or three times.

KENTON:     (*Looking at CLIVE*) That's what I wanted to know, sir.

CLIVE: (*Moving towards the INSPECTOR: just a faint suggestion of irritation*) Look, Inspector, if there's anything at the back of your mind ...

KENTON: (*Casually, quite pleasant*) There's nothing at the back of my mind, sir. I've one or two questions I'd like to ask you but they're not terribly important – they can wait.

CLIVE: No. No, go ahead.

KENTON: (*With a glance at LAURENCE*) They're rather personal questions, Mr Freeman. Perhaps I'd better ...

CLIVE: That's all right. You can say what you'd like in front of Mr Hudson – he's my lawyer as well as being a friend.

KENTON: Well – what made you leave Prescott, sir?

CLIVE: (*Surprised by the question*) What made me leave Prescott?

KENTON: Yes. You were making quite a reputation for yourself.

CLIVE: I was making seventeen hundred a year. I pay that in surtax.

KENTON: I see, sir.

CLIVE: However, to be truthful, that wasn't the only reason. I was tired of doing research work and I wanted to start a business of my own.

KENTON: I understand that when you left Prescott you were engaged on certain scientific investigations ...

CLIVE: I was working on a moulding process rather on the lines of the Riverdale Press. I suppose you could call that a scientific investigation.

KENTON: Well, let's put it another way, sir. I understand the work you did at Prescott was – well, top secret.

85

CLIVE: Everything they do at Prescott is top secret. There's even an element of mystery about the steak and kidney pie.

KENTON: (*Smiling*) Well, just one more question, Mr Freeman. Did Dr Bramwell-Cane ever express an interest in (*He stops: something has caught his eye on the carpet. He stoops down and picks up a button*) I think someone's lost a button, sir.

CLIVE: Oh … (*Takes the button from KENTON*) Oh, thank you.

*LAURENCE looks across at CLIVE as he examines the button. CLIVE looks down at his jacket, so does LAURENCE. Neither of them has lost a button.*

CLIVE: (*Hesitant, to KENTON*) It's possibly off one of my other suits.

LAURENCE: (*Purposely attempting to distract KENTON's attention from the button*) What were you saying, Inspector? Did Dr Bramwell-Cane …

KENTON: (*Still looking at the button, to CLIVE*) I was saying, did Dr Bramwell-Cane ever express an interest in your work, sir?

CLIVE: We were both metallurgical chemists. We both worked at Prescott. There is a certain degree of co-operation in Government departments, Inspector.

KENTON: (*Pleasantly*) Thank you, sir – you've answered my question.

*LUCY enters from the Hall. She has just arrived and is replacing the front door key in her handbag.*

LUCY: Good evening, Inspector.

KENTON: (*Turning*) Oh, good evening, Mrs Freeman.

*CLIVE moves towards LUCY.*

CLIVE:    There's no news, Lucy. (*Significantly*) The Inspector just happened to be passing …

LUCY:    Oh, I see.

KENTON:    (*Looking at LUCY, then across at CLIVE*) Well, goodnight, sir, and thank you for that information – to say nothing of the drink.

CLIVE:    Goodnight, Inspector.

KENTON:    (*To LAURENCE*) Goodbye, Mr Hudson.

*LAURENCE nods to the INSPECTOR.*

KENTON:    Goodnight, Mrs Freeman.

LUCY:    (*Looking at LAURENCE*) Goodnight.

*KENTON goes out, followed by CLIVE. LUCY immediately crosses to LAURENCE.*

LUCY:    (*Anxiously*) Laurence, what happened?

LAURENCE:    (*Shaking his head*) Nothing. He didn't turn up.

LUCY:    (*Amazed*) What do you mean?

LAURENCE:    (*Obviously worried, faintly on edge*) The man didn't turn up, Lucy – no one came …

*LAURENCE crosses to the drinks table and begins to mix himself a drink. LUCY sinks down onto the arm of the settee, still looking at LAURENCE.*

LAURENCE:    Would you like a drink?

*LUCY shakes her head.*

LAURENCE:    Do you mind if I help myself?

LUCY:    (*Watching LAURENCE, faintly puzzled*) No, of course not.

*CLIVE enters. He is examining the button. LUCY crosses over to CLIVE.*

LUCY:    Clive, Laurence says no one came tonight – nothing happened?

87

CLIVE:    (*Putting the button into his pocket*) Yes, that's true, Lucy.

LUCY:    You mean you've been here all the time – just waiting?

CLIVE:    What else could we do?

LUCY:    You could have tried to have got in touch with Pelford!

CLIVE:    We have been trying. I've been on the phone since ten o'clock.

*CLIVE looks at LUCY then crosses to the desk and picks up the telephone again. LUCY looks at CLIVE, then across to LAURENCE. LAURENCE drops his eyes and looks at the glass in his hand. LUCY looks faintly puzzled.*


CUT TO:   Henshaw Wood.

NELSON's body is lying in the undergrowth of Henshaw Wood. Traffic can be heard in the background travelling along the main road to London. It is early morning, but the light is fairly strong. The birds are singing in the wood. *After a moment NELSON's right arm moves slightly, then his head moves, then his body stirs and he slowly raises himself up from the ground, and takes stock of his surroundings. For a moment he looks dazed and completely bewildered. He feels the back of his head and quickly winces with pain. Gradually he regains complete consciousness and rises to his feet, holding on to the branches of the undergrowth for support. He stands quite still, apparently still feeling the effect of CLIVE's knockout blow. It is obvious that he has not suffered any ill effects from the revolver shot. (There is a button missing off his coat). After a little while he glances at his watch, slowly collects his hat and walking-stick, and is about to move off when he notices the revolver on the ground. He stoops down, picks it up, puts it in his pocket, and then with very uncertain steps, makes his way towards the bank and the main road.*

CUT TO: *The Main Road as Nelson comes into view over the top of the bank. A lorry can be seen approaching in the distance. NELSON sees the lorry and moves into the middle of the road. As the lorry draws nearer, he starts to wave his arms. The lorry reaches NELSON and finally pulls up.*

CUT TO: *FRED WADE, the lorry-driver, staring down at NELSON from his cabin.*

FRED:      D'you wan' a lift?

NELSON: (*Still a little dazed*) Are you going to London?

FRED:      No, I'm going to Slough, if that's any use to you.

NELSON: Yes. Yes, thank you very much.

*After an unsuccessful attempt NELSON finally climbs into the cabin of the lorry. FRED looks at NELSON with obvious curiosity.*

FRED:      You're in a bit of a bad way, chum. What happened?

NELSON: I had an accident.

FRED:      What – a car accident?

NELSON: No, I was on a bicycle … Something happened to the front wheel … It was entirely my own fault.

FRED:      (*A little surprised by the explanation*) Oh.

NELSON: You must excuse me. I'm still a little bit confused.

*FRED changes gear and lets out the clutch.*

FRED:      Yes, sure … You'll soon be all right, mate …

NELSON: (*Looking at Fred with the suggestion of a smile*) I hope so.

CUT TO: The Drawing Room at Amberley. Later the same morning.

*The curtains are drawn back and the French windows open. CLIVE enters from the hall. He is holding a newspaper and is obviously searching for a possible report on the discovery of NELSON in Henshaw Wood. He finishes with the newspaper, and crosses to the desk. LAURENCE enters the room through the French windows.*

CLIVE:       Oh, hello, Laurence! I've been looking for you.

LAURENCE:    I've been down to the village to see about the car.

CLIVE:       Is it all right, now?

LAURENCE:    It soon will be. They're changing the wheel. They said they'd deliver it in about half an hour.

CLIVE:       (*A shade nervously*) There's nothing in the papers.

LAURENCE:    I didn't think there would be. It's far too soon. (*He moves towards CLIVE*) It might be days before they find him. (*Looking at CLIVE*) Have you had any breakfast this morning?

CLIVE:       No.

LAURENCE:    I didn't think you had. (*He indicates the telephone*) Have you tried to get Pelford?

CLIVE:       Yes, I've been trying since eight o'clock – there's still no reply.

LAURENCE:    Where's Lucy?

CLIVE:       She's in her room. She'll be down in a minute.

*LAURENCE glances at his wristlet watch.*

90

LAURENCE: I've got an appointment in Town at eleven o'clock. If you want me or anything happens during the day, give me a ring at the office. I shall be there until five.

CLIVE: Right. (*A moment, quietly, looking at LAURENCE*) Laurence …

LAURENCE: Yes?

CLIVE: (*After a momentary hesitation*) I told Lucy.

LAURENCE: (*Surprised*) When?

CLIVE: Last night – or rather this morning. She came to my room and …

LAURENCE: (*Angrily*) Why? Why did you tell her? I thought we'd agreed …

CLIVE: I had to tell her! She knew something was the matter. She sensed it. I don't know why, or how, but …

LAURENCE: (*Quietly*) All right, so you've told her. What did she say?

CLIVE: At first she just couldn't believe it. She couldn't understand why we didn't go to the police. When I told her why she – (*Hesitates*) made a suggestion, Laurence. I think it's a very good one.

LAURENCE: What is it?

*LUCY enters from the hall and LAURENCE turns towards her.*

LUCY: (*To LAURENCE*) I suggested I went to Pelford – that I was the one that complained and that no-one turned up.

LAURENCE: (*A moment: then obviously impressed*) I think that's a very good idea, Lucy! (*To CLIVE*) Now why didn't we think of that,

CLIVE: Clive? It's far more likely to convince him than a telephone call.

CLIVE: Well – that's what I thought.

LUCY: After all, I saw Pelford. It was through me that the arrangements were made in the first place.

LAURENCE: Exactly! Besides you could take the attitude that you stuck to your side of the bargain by not going to the police, why haven't they stuck to theirs? (*A nod*) It's a very good idea, Lucy.

CLIVE: You'd better see Pelford this morning, darling. I'll pick you up at Laurence's office at one o'clock.

LUCY: (*Looking at CLIVE*) Yes, all right. I'd better tell Anna we shall be out all day. (*She turns towards the door*).

LAURENCE: (*Stopping her*) Lucy, did Clive tell you about the receipt we found on Nelson?

LUCY: Yes, he did.

LAURENCE: Have you ever heard of this man, Stevens?

LUCY: Yes, I've been to him – once.

LAURENCE: What's he like?

LUCY: You mean – as a dentist?

LAURENCE: No. No, as a person.

LUCY: Quite young, extremely good looking. (*Thoughtfully*) I heard something about him a little while ago – I've been trying to think what it was …

LAURENCE: What do you mean you heard something – a rumour of some kind?

LUCY: (*Trying to recall what she has heard*) Yes. Lady Barstow – Barbara – told me something about him. Oh, dear – what on earth was it?

CLIVE: Well, if Barbara told you about it, it probably wasn't true anyway.

*The telephone rings. CLIVE looks at LAURENCE then picks up the receiver. LAURENCE and LUCY stand watching CLIVE, listening to the conversation.*

CLIVE: (*On the phone*) Hello? Beacherscross 189 …

KENTON: (*On the other end*) Mr Freeman?

CLIVE: Yes.

KENTON: Inspector Kenton, sir.

CLIVE: Oh, good morning, Inspector. (*He looks up at LAURENCE*)

KENTON: Mr Freeman, Superintendent Wilde would like to see you sometime today. Would two o'clock this afternoon be convenient?

CLIVE: (*Hesitant*) Well, I was going up to Town this morning …

KENTON: Oh, dear. It's rather important, sir.

CLIVE: Well – all right, Inspector. Two o'clock.

KENTON: Thank you, sir. (*Replaces receiver*)

*CLIVE replaces the receiver.*

CLIVE: (*To LAURENCE and LUCY*) It was Kenton. Wilde wants to see me. (*To LUCY*) I'm afraid you'll have to come back from Town on the train, Lucy.

LUCY: (*Nodding*) All right.

LAURENCE: Do you think they've found Nelson?

CLIVE: (*After a moment, thoughtfully*) I don't know, Laurence …

CUT TO: ROBERT STEVENS' Consulting Room at South Bank Chambers, Kingsbridge.

The room is a typical dentist's consulting room – a dentist's chair, X-ray apparatus, desk with telephone, small box file, notepaper, etc.

*ROBERT STEVENS is sitting in a swivel chair at the desk, studying a series of X-ray plates. He is a very good-looking man in his late twenties. He wears a collar-high white jacket and dark trousers. NURSE LYNN enters the consulting room. She is a rather severe looking brunette. STEVENS swings round and faces her.*

LYNN: She's arrived.

STEVENS: (*A shade annoyed, nodding*) All right – send her in. You know what to do?

*LYNN nods and goes out. STEVENS rises and crosses towards the door. After a moment RUTH CALTHORPE enters the consulting room. She looks a little older than the last time we saw her, and a shade worried. She quietly closes the door and faces STEVENS.*

RUTH: Robert, I'm sorry to disturb you. I know you're frightfully busy, and you don't like me to come here, but – I haven't heard from you, Robert, not for over a fortnight.

STEVENS: Ruth, I've been madly busy. You know what it is …

RUTH: (*Hurt*) You could have telephoned. You could have written me a note.

STEVENS: I did telephone.

RUTH: (*Anxiously*) When?

STEVENS: (*Obviously lying*) Oh – a few days ago. Someone – one of the other teachers – said you weren't available, so naturally I thought …

RUTH: (*Shaking her head*) I don't believe you.

STEVENS:     (*Annoyed*) All right, you don't believe me.

RUTH:        Robert, did you – did you telephone?

STEVENS:     Of course I did. Now look, Ruth, I've told you before, it's not possible to see you every week. Don't forget I've got the other practice to look after as well as this …

RUTH:        Yes, I know, but … Robert, I'm awfully worried. Someone else came to see me this morning.

STEVENS:     Someone else? What do you mean?

RUTH:        Well, Inspector Kenton interviewed me last week. I told you. It was the second time he'd …

STEVENS:     Yes. Yes, I know. But what about this morning?

RUTH:        A man called Wilde visited the school. He said he was from Scotland Yard. He spoke to Miss Browning – the Headmistress – and then questioned me. I was with him nearly half an hour.

*STEVENS takes hold of her arm. His attitude is definitely friendlier.*

STEVENS:     Well, that's all right, Ruth. There's nothing to worry about. I told you that sort of thing would happen.

RUTH:        You also told me it would all be over in three or four days. You said Janet would be back with her parents …

STEVENS:     Ruth, dear … I've told you, Janet's perfectly all right. Why, you've spoken to her yourself on the telephone – you know she's all right. It won't be long now before it's all over, I promise you. (*He draws her*

95

|          | *towards him*) Now what did this man Wilde say to you? |
| RUTH: | He asked me all the usual questions. What time did I leave the school? … What did Janet say to me? I told him exactly what I told Kenton. |
| STEVENS: | Nothing else – he didn't say anything else? |
| RUTH: | No. (*A thought*) Oh, he asked me if I was engaged. |
| STEVENS: | (*Surprised*) Engaged? Engaged to be married? |
| RUTH: | Yes. |
| STEVENS: | Why did he ask you that? |
| RUTH: | I don't know. |
| STEVENS: | What did you tell him? |
| RUTH: | I told him I wasn't – not officially. |
| STEVENS: | (*Hesitating*) You didn't mention … |
| RUTH: | (*Facing him*) I didn't say anything about you, Robert – if that's what you're thinking. |
| STEVENS: | That's not what I was thinking at all, Ruth. (*Holds her arms and looks at her*) You know you'll have to start trusting me, darling. Just a little bit. (*He draws her towards him and kisses her*) |
| RUTH: | (*Quite simply*) It isn't really necessary, you know. |
| STEVENS: | (*Puzzled*) What do you mean? |
| RUTH: | (*Shaking her head*) It isn't necessary for me to trust you, Robert. I'm in love with you. (*Looks at him*) You're quite safe. I shan't let you down. |

STEVENS:     Ruth, it isn't a question of letting me
             down. You went into this with your eyes
             open. You agreed …
RUTH:        (*Interrupting him*) You told me the whole
             thing would last two or three days. Four at
             the outside. It's now almost …
STEVENS:     Yes. Yes, I know, and I'm just as worried
             by that aspect of it as you are. But I've
             explained before, darling, I'm not the only
             one involved in this.

*The door opens and NURSE LYNN enters.*

STEVENS:     Once I get … (*Breaks off, moves away
             from RUTH and looks towards LYNN*)
             Yes, Nurse?
LYNN:        There are three patients in the waiting
             room, sir. And Dr Lester's coming at two
             o'clock.
STEVENS:     Yes, all right, Nurse.

*LYNN stands in the open doorway, waiting for Ruth to
leave. STEVENS smiles at RUTH, takes her hand and
gives it a gentle squeeze.*

STEVENS:     I'll phone you tomorrow morning, Ruth.
             We'll fix something up for the weekend.
RUTH:        Is that a promise?
STEVENS:     Yes, of course, darling.
RUTH:        Try and phone before half past ten if you
             can.
STEVENS:     (*Smiling at her*) I'll try, dear.

*RUTH gives a little smile and goes out. LYNN looks at
STEVENS then closes the door. As the door closes
STEVENS' expression changes. He crosses to the desk and
sits down in the swivel chair. He picks up a packet of
cigarettes, extracts a cigarette from the packet and puts it
in his mouth. He swings round in the chair, facing the*

*door, takes a lighter from his pocket, flicks it and lights the cigarette. The charm has faded.*

CUT TO: *A taxi arrives at the entrance to Amberley at the same time as a police car exits from the drive. The taxi pulls to one side to allow the police car to pass. LUCY is in the taxi and she leans forward slightly to see the occupants of the other car. They are DETECTIVE INSPECTOR KENTON and SUPERINTENDENT WILDE. KENTON notices LUCY and raises his hat. The police car disappears, and the taxi goes through the gates and continues up the drive towards the house.*

CUT TO: *The taxi arrives at the house. LUCY gets out and pays the driver. CLIVE is standing on the steps in front of the house waiting for LUCY. As she comes up the steps he moves down, takes hold of her arm and together they go into the house.*

CUT TO:   The Hall at Amberley.
A rather delightful hall with a winding staircase leading upstairs. Doors leading to study, dining room, drawing room, etc.
*CLIVE and LUCY come through the front door into the hall. LUCY takes off her hat during the following dialogue.*

CLIVE:     Kenton's only just left, I expect you saw the car.
LUCY:      Yes.
CLIVE:     They've been here since two o'clock.
LUCY:      (*Quietly*) Have they found him?
CLIVE:     No. Not yet. What happened, Lucy? Did you see Pelford?
*They cross into the drawing room.*

98

LUCY: *(As she comes into the room)* There was no sign of Pelford, so I called round again this afternoon. The studio was deserted. The woman on the floor above told me that no-one's been near the place for two or three days.

CLIVE: *(Softly, obviously worried)* Oh …

LUCY: I think he's gone for good, Clive, because the case had disappeared.

CLIVE: Which case?

LUCY: There was a showcase on the wall near the entrance to the studio. I noticed it the first time I went there. It wasn't there this morning.

CLIVE: I don't like the sound of this, Lucy.

LUCY: No, neither does Laurence. I saw him just before I left Town. He's very worried.

CLIVE: You see, Pelford's our only contact. If we can't find Pelford how can we convince them that Nelson didn't show up?

LUCY: Perhaps you can't convince them.

CLIVE: What do you mean?

LUCY: Perhaps they already know about Nelson?

CLIVE: How can they know? The body hasn't been found yet. That's the whole point. We've got to find Pelford before the body's discovered.

*LUCY crosses and presses the bell by the side of the writing bureau.*

LUCY: *(Turning)* What did the Superintendent want?

CLIVE: I don't know. I'm damned if I know. He was here an hour and a half, and he only mentioned Janet once, and that was just as he was leaving.

LUCY: Well – what did he talk about?

CLIVE: He talked about me and Prescott most of the time.

LUCY: Prescott?

99

CLIVE:   Yes. He wanted to know exactly what I did at Prescott, why I left there … why I started a business of my own.

LUCY:    But what's all that got to do with Janet?

CLIVE:   (*Shaking his head*) I don't know, but they must think it's important. Kenton's questioned me before about Prescott.

LUCY:    Clive, coming back in the train this afternoon, I started thinking about last night.

CLIVE:   Well?

LUCYL    How long was Nelson here before … the accident happened?

CLIVE:   Oh, only a matter of minutes. Why?

LUCY:    Didn't he say anything?

CLIVE:   Yes, I've told you. He said he wanted certain information from me. He said if I gave him the information, they'd return Janet.

LUCY:    But didn't he tell you what the information was?

CLIVE:   No. Just at that moment Laurence dropped his glasses.

LUCY:    And you've no idea what he was referring to?

CLIVE:   Not the slightest. I wish to God I had.

LUCY:    D'you think it was anything to do with Prescott?

*CLIVE looks at LUCY and hesitates a moment.*

CLIVE:   I think it must have been.

LUCY:    Clive, we were very happy when you were doing research. A great deal happier than we've been since. But you never talked a great deal about it. You never told me what went on at Prescott.

CLIVE:   I was working on a moulding process most of the time, a development of the Riverdale Press.

LUCY:     Was it important work?

CLIVE:    Of course. Everything they do at Prescott is important.

LUCY:     No, I didn't mean that.

CLIVE:    What did you mean?

LUCY:     I meant was it … (*Faces him*) Was it a secret process? Have you information about it which would be of value to someone else?

CLIVE:    No … Most of the work I did they've scrapped, anyway. They're working on entirely different lines now. That's one of the reasons why I left, Lucy. Miller and I just didn't agree.

LUCY:     Did you tell Wilde this, this afternoon?

CLIVE:    I told him about the process. I didn't say anything about Miller. Wilde's a curious character, he appeared to understand all the technical …

*CLIVE breaks off as ANNA enters the room.*

ANNA:     (*To LUCY*) Did you ring, Mrs Freeman?

LUCY:     (*Turning*) Oh, yes, Anna. I'd like some tea.

ANNA:     (*To CLIVE*) Mr Freeman?

CLIVE:    No, thank you, nothing for me.

ANNA:     (*To LUCY*) Lady Barstow called while you were out, madam. (*To CLIVE*) I didn't disturb you, sir, you were with the Inspector.

CLIVE:    Thank you, Anna.

LUCY:     What did she want this time?

ANNA:     She borrowed some cocktail mats, madam. She's returning them next week.

CLIVE:    Why the devil she doesn't come and live with us I don't know!

ANNA:     (*Smiling*) Oh, no, please, not that, Mr Freeman!

LUCY:     (*With a quiet smile, dismissing ANNA*) All right, Anna.

101

ANNA:     (*To CLIVE*) And she asked me to tell you that
          … she was right about the dentist.
LUCY:     She was right about the dentist?
ANNA:     Yes, Mrs Freeman. I don't know what she
          meant, I'm sure.
LUCY:     (*Quietly*) Thank you, Anna.
*ANNA goes out.*
LUCY:     (*To CLIVE*) What did Barbara mean?
CLIVE:    You remember … she was taking about
          Stevens. She couldn't make up her mind
          whether he'd recommended Pelford or not?
LUCY:     (*Her thoughts elsewhere*) Oh, I see.
CLIVE:    (*Looking at LUCY, curious*) What is it, Lucy?
LUCY:     (*Thoughtfully*) You remember, this morning I
          said Barbara told me something else about
          Stevens, but I couldn't remember what it was.
CLIVE:    Yes.
LUCY:     I've just remembered. Someone told her that he
          was friendly with Miss Calthorpe.
CLIVE:    (*Surprised*) Miss Calthorpe?
LUCY:     Yes.
CLIVE:    But I thought Stevens was a good-looking
          young man, a bit of a heart throb?
LUCY:     He is …
CLIVE:    Well, I can hardly imagine a good-looking
          young chap falling for anyone like Ruth
          Calthorpe … (*Quietly*) Still, it might be a very
          good idea if I had a word with Stevens. After
          all, Nelson was a patient of his. If we could get
          Nelson's address …
LUCY:     It might lead us to Pelford.
CLIVE:    Exactly.
*CLIVE crosses to the desk and picks up the local telephone
directory.*

CLIVE:    What's his initials?

LUCY:    I think it's R.C. Robert …

*CLIVE opens the book and looks down the pages.*

LUCY:    Clive, don't you think there's something rather odd about this Stevens business?

CLIVE:    Yes, I do.

LUCY:    Whichever way you look at it there are three important points. We just can't afford to ignore them.

CLIVE:    One: Nelson was a patient of his …

LUCY:    Two: there's a rumour that he's friendly with Miss Calthorpe.

CLIVE:    And three: it was Stevens that mentioned Pelford to Barbara in the first place.

LUCY:    Yes.

CLIVE:    Well, we'll take a look at this Mr Stevens and see what he's got to say. (*He looks at the directory*) This is it: Robert C. Stevens, L.D.S., South Bank Chambers, Kingsdown …

LUCY:    That's it.

CLIVE:    … Kingsdown 836 …

*CLIVE puts down the directory, turns towards the desk and picks up the telephone and dials the number. He stands for a moment, listening to the number ringing out, looking at LUCY.*

LYNN:    (*On the other end of the line*) … Kingsdown 836 …

CLIVE:    Good afternoon … My name is Freeman. I want to make an appointment to see Mr Stevens.

LYNN:    Have you seen Mr Stevens before?

CLIVE:    No, but my wife's a patient of his. I've had rather a bad toothache for the last two or three

days and I was wondering if Mr Stevens would
be kind enough to …

LYNN: (*Interrupting him*) Just a moment please.

*There is a pause.*

LUCY: (*To CLIVE*)   What's happening?

CLIVE: I don't know. She's probably having a word
with him.

*A second pause.*

LYNN: (*On the other end*) Hello …

CLIVE: Yes?

LYNN: Did you say Mr Freeman?

CLIVE: Yes … Amberley, Connaught Avenue.

LYNN: Well – would nine-thirty tomorrow morning be
any use to you?

CLIVE: Yes, that would do nicely. Thank you very
much.

LYNN: You have the address?

CLIVE: Yes – South Bank Chambers.

LYNN: What initials, Mr Freeman?

CLIVE: C – for Clive.

LYNN: Thank you.  Goodbye.

CLIVE: Goodbye. (*He replaces the receiver and looks
at LUCY*)

LUCY: Well?

CLIVE: (*Quietly*) Nine-thirty tomorrow morning …


CUT TO:  ROBERT STEVENS' Surgery.

*STEVENS is standing by a wash basin rinsing his hands.
He takes a bottle of lotion from the ledge above the basin,
pours a little of the lotion over his hands and then dries
them on a towel.*

STEVENS: (*To CLIVE*) I think you'll find that
dressing should do the trick … although
I'm quite surprised it's given you quite so

104

much trouble, Mr Freeman. It's a reasonably sound tooth. It would be a pity for you to lose it.

*He turns and moves to the dental chair. CLIVE is sitting in the chair. STEVENS stands looking down at him.*

CLIVE: I'm very grateful to you for fitting me in like this.

STEVENS: Not at all. (*He leans forwards, touches CLIVE's mouth, looks at the tooth*) Yes, I think that'll be all right in a minute or two.

CLIVE: Thank you.

STEVENS: (*Pleasantly*) I believe your wife came to see me about twelve months ago?

CLIVE: Yes, she did. We were recommended to you by a Mr Nelson.

STEVENS: Mr Nelson?

CLIVE: Yes.

STEVENS: Is he a patient of mine?

CLIVE: Yes, so I understand.

STEVENS: Nelson? That's very odd. I don't seem to recall the name. Does he live in Kingsdown?

*NURSE LYNN enters.*

CLIVE: (*Hesitant*) I'm not sure …

STEVENS: (*Turning towards LYNN*) Yes, Nurse?

LYNN: Dr Craig would like a word with you, sir. He's in the Waiting Room.

STEVENS: Yes, certainly. (*To CLIVE*) Excuse me. (*He moves to the door. To LYNN, pleasantly*) Oh, Nurse … do we know a Mr Nelson?

LYNN: (*Thoughtfully*) No … No, I don't think so.

STEVENS:     (*Shaking his head, smiling*) I couldn't
             recall the name. (*To CLIVE*) I shan't be a
             minute Mr Freeman.

*STEVENS goes out of the room. NURSE LYNN crosses to
the desk, picks up the appointment book and consults it.
CLIVE sits in the chair, watching her. After a moment she
smiles at CLIVE, puts down the book and goes out of the
room. CLIVE turns, and looks towards the door, he
hesitates, then with his eyes still on the door he rises from
the chair and crosses to the desk. He bends down and
quietly looks through the alphabetical box-index file.
Suddenly he finds the card he is looking for. He takes a
diary from his pocket and quickly copies the details from
the card into the diary. Having completed this he puts the
card back into the box-file and returns to the chair. The
moment he sits down the door opens and STEVENS
returns. He crosses to CLIVE.*

STEVENS:     Sorry about that. (*He touches CLIVE's
             mouth, looks at the filling, picks up an
             instrument and gently touches the
             tooth*) That's all right …

*He stands back and CLIVE rises from the chair.*

CLIVE:       Thank you very much.

*They shake hands.*

STEVENS:     Not at all. (*Crossing towards the door*) If
             you do get any trouble with it, let me
             know. (*Smiling*) But I don't think you will.

*STEVENS opens the door and with a nod CLIVE goes out.
STEVENS returns to the desk, sits down in the swivel
chair, and draws the box-file towards him. He looks at the
file for a moment, smiling to himself, then he flicks his
fingers through the file and takes out the card, then still
smiling, tears it into tiny pieces, and drops it into the*

106

*waste-paper basket. The door opens and LYNN enters. She crosses to the desk.*

LYNN:     (*Looking down at STEVENS*) Well?

*STEVENS looks up at her and nods his head.*

STEVENS:  He got what he came for.


CUT TO:   *CLIVE's car drives up to the main entrance of Amberley. A police car is parked outside of the door. CLIVE gets out of the Bentley and with a brief nod to the uniformed driver sitting in the police car, he crosses to the front door and lets himself into the house.*


CUT TO:   The Hall of Amberley.

*LUCY comes out of the drawing room and joins CLIVE near the front door.*

LUCY:     (*Quietly*) The Inspector's here.

CLIVE:    Yes, I know. (*Nodding towards the door*) I've seen the car. What does he want?

LUCY:     I don't know. I told him you weren't in, but he asked if he could wait. He's been here about twenty minutes.

*CLIVE nods and moves towards the drawing room.*

LUCY:     (*Holding on to his arm*) Did you see Stevens?

CLIVE:    (*Nodding, quietly*) Yes. I'll tell you about it later.

*CLIVE goes into the drawing room where DETECTIVE INSPECTOR KENTON is sitting on the settee, glancing at a glossy magazine. He rises as CLIVE enters and picks up a large envelope which is on the arm of the settee.*

CLIVE:    Sorry to have kept you waiting, Inspector. I had a dentist's appointment.

KENTON:   So I understand, sir. I trust it wasn't too painful?

107

CLIVE: It's been aching for two days and the confounded thing stopped the moment I sat in the chair.

KENTON: (*Smiling*) That's usually the case, sir.

CLIVE: Well – what can I do for you?

KENTON: (*A shade too casual*) I don't know that you can do anything for us, sir. It's just a routine inquiry.

CLIVE: Oh. Well … go ahead.

*KENTON opens the envelope and takes out a very large glossy photograph.*

KENTON: I've got a photograph here, Mr Freeman. I'd like you to take a look at it.

*THE INSPECTOR hands CLIVE the photograph. CLIVE looks at it and after a moment looks up.*

CLIVE: Well, Inspector?

KENTON: Have you seen that man before, sir?

CLIVE: (*After a moment*) No. Never.

KENTON: (*Watching CLIVE*) You're quite sure, Mr Freeman?

CLIVE: Yes, I'm quite sure. Why do you ask?

KENTON: We found his body in Henshaw Wood late last night. He was murdered.

*CLIVE looks at the INSPECTOR, then down at the photograph. The photograph is of NELSON. He is seen lying on his back, eyes closed, in what appears to be part of a densely wooded copse. He is dressed precisely the same as the last time we saw him. The hat, stick and revolver are by the side of the body.*

# END OF EPISODE THREE

# EPISODE FOUR

OPEN TO:     The Drawing Room at Amberley.

*DETECTIVE INSPECTOR KENTON is facing CLIVE who is looking down at the photograph in his hand.*

KENTON: Have you seen that man before, sir?

CLIVE:     (*After a moment*) No; never …

KENTON:(*Watching him*) You're quite sure, Mr Freeman?

CLIVE:     Yes, I'm quite sure. Why do you ask?

KENTON: We found his body in Henshaw Wood late last night. He was murdered.

*CLIVE looks at the INSPECTOR then down at the photograph.*

CLIVE:     (*Quietly*) I've never seen him before …

*LUCY enters from the hall.*

KENTON:(*Taking the photograph from CLIVE*) Thank you, sir. (*He turns towards LUCY*) Ah, Mrs Freeman! Would you take a look at this photograph, please, and tell me if you recognise the man?

*Somewhat puzzled LUCY takes the photograph from the Inspector and looks at it.*

LUCY:     (*After a moment*) Who is he?

KENTON: We don't know. He was found last night in Henshaw Wood.

CLIVE:     (*Surprised and puzzled*) You don't know? You mean … you don't know who he is?

KENTON:(*Quietly, looking at CLIVE*) No, sir. That's the point of the photograph. We're trying to identify him.

CLIVE:     But wasn't there anything on him … in his pockets … that identified him?

KENTON: (*Innocently*) What do you mean, sir?

CLIVE:     Well, hadn't he a wallet or …

KENTON: Yes?

CLIVE: … Or anything like that?

KENTON: (*Shaking his head*) His pockets were empty. He hadn't even a handkerchief on him.

CLIVE: Oh, I see.

LUCY: Well … what made you think we might be able to identify him, Inspector?

KENTON: I don't know that I did think that, Mr Freeman. It's a routine enquiry. We're showing the photograph to lots of people.

LUCY: Oh …

KENTON: But naturally we're wondering if the murder was connected with the disappearance of your daughter.

CLIVE: And do you think it is?

KENTON: (*Thoughtfully*) It's too early to say, sir. (*Pleasantly*) Well, thank you, Mr Freeman. It's very good of you to … (*Stops, apparently having remembered something*) Oh, by the way … do you remember the button I found, the night Mr Hudson was here?

CLIVE: Yes, it was off my sports jacket.

KENTON: Oh, was it! Well, that's what I wanted to know. (*Points to the photograph*) There's a button missing off his coat and it just crossed my mind that …

CLIVE: The one you found was off my sports jacket. Anna sewed it on for me …

KENTON: (*Smiling, apparently quite convinced*) Thank you, sir.

*ANNA enters from the hall with LAURENCE HUDSON.*

ANNA: Mr Hudson, sir.

CLIVE: Come in, Laurence.

*LAURENCE comes into the room. He is wearing an overcoat and carries his hat and a morning newspaper.*

KENTON: (*To LUCY*) Goodbye, Mrs Freeman.

LUCY: Goodbye, Inspector.

KENTON: (*To CLIVE*) Goodbye, sir.

CLIVE: Goodbye, Inspector. (*To ANNA*) The Inspector's leaving, Anna.

*KENTON nods to LAURENCE and goes out with ANNA.*

CLIVE: (*To LAURENCE*) Laurence, this is a surprise ... we weren't expecting you.

LAURENCE: I'm on my way up north. I've got an appointment in Oxford. (*He looks towards the door, waits for the closing of the front door before speaking again. Then he turns to CLIVE and LUCY and holds out the newspaper*) Have you seen this?

CLIVE: No ...

LAURENCE: They've found him.

CLIVE: (*Nodding towards the door*) Yes, I know ... that's why he was here.

*LUCY takes the newspaper from LAURENCE.*

LUCY: What does it say?

LAURENCE: ... It just says the body of a man was found in Henshaw Wood early this morning. There's no details. (*A note of tenseness in his voice*) What did Kenton say?

CLIVE: He brought a photograph of the body. He wanted to know if we could identify him.

LUCY: (*To LAURENCE, looking up from the newspaper*) They don't know who he is.

LAURENCE: (*Puzzled*) What do you mean?

CLIVE: There was nothing on the body ... No wallet, no receipt, nothing ...

LAURENCE: (*To CLIVE*) But I put the wallet back in his pocket, and the receipt. You saw me do it!

CLIVE: Yes, I know. Someone must have gone through his pockets after we left him.

LUCY: (*To LAURENCE*) Was there any money in the wallet?

LAURENCE: Yes, about ten or twelve pounds, and some foreign currency. (*To CLIVE*) What else did Kenton say?

CLIVE: He mentioned the button. It was off Nelson's overcoat.

LAURENCE: Oh, my God ...

CLIVE: It's all right. I told him it was off my sports jacket.

LUCY: You also told him Anna sewed it on for you. Supposing he questions her?

CLIVE: I pulled a button off my jacket last night. She sewed it on for me this morning.

LAURENCE: (*Indicating newspaper*) You know it's an extraordinary thing. I've been expecting this ever since it happened, and yet when I read about it ... it gave me quite a shock ...

LUCY: (*To CLIVE*) Clive, what happened this morning? Did you see Stevens?

*LAURENCE looks at LUCY, obviously surprised.*

LAURENCE: Stevens ... the dentist?

LUCY: Yes, Clive had an appointment with him.

CLIVE: (*Nodding*) Yes, I saw him. He said he'd never heard of Nelson.

LAURENCE: But he must have heard of him, otherwise how the devil did the receipt ...

114

| | |
|---|---|
| CLIVE: | He'd heard of him all right. He went out of the room for a few minutes and I looked through his file. (*Takes his diary out of his pocket*) I found Nelson's address. (*Reading from the diary*) Ashtree Cottage, Lower Meldon, Hertfordshire. |
| LUCY: | Lower Meldon? Where's that? |
| LAURENCE: | I think it's near Aylesbury, I'm not sure. |
| CLIVE: | Yes, it's about five or ten miles from Aylesbury. |
| LAURENCE: | (*Puzzled, to CLIVE*) You say, Stevens said he'd never heard of Nelson? |
| CLIVE: | Yes. He was quite definite about it. He asked the nurse. She said she'd never heard of him, either. |
| LAURENCE: | I don't understand this. Why should Stevens lie? Just because Nelson was a patient of his it doesn't mean to say … |
| CLIVE: | (*Shaking his head*) If you ask me, Stevens knew why I went there this morning. He knew why I was interested in Nelson. |
| LAURENCE: | You mean he's mixed up in this? |
| CLIVE: | Yes. |
| LUCY: | (*To LAURENCE*) Did you know he was friendly with Miss Calthorpe? |
| LAURENCE: | What – the schoolmistress? |
| LUCY: | Yes. |
| LAURENCE: | No, I didn't know that. |
| CLIVE: | That's just a rumour, but the point is this. I got what I went for – which was Nelson's address. Now what do we do with it? |
| LAURENCE: | (*Hesitant, obviously worried*) I think you'd better give it to Superintendent Wilde … |

CLIVE: And tell him the whole story?

LAURENCE: Yes, I think so, Clive.

LUCY: (*Facing LAURENCE*) I don't agree. I can see your point of view, Laurence. I can understand why you're worried about this business but …

LAURENCE: (*Interrupting her, but not unfriendly*) Well – what do <u>you</u> want to do, Lucy?

*CLIVE and LAURENCE turn towards Lucy; she looks worried for a moment; a shade uncertain of herself.*

CLIVE: (*To LUCY*) Well?

LUCY: (*A moment*) I think we ought to go to this place – Lower Meldon. Nelson obviously knew where Janet was, and in my opinion …

CLIVE: (*Surprised*) You think she's at the cottage?

LUCY: Well, she's somewhere, isn't she, Clive? Why not Nelson's cottage?

CLIVE: (*To LAURENCE*) What do you think, Laurence?

LAURENCE: (*Thoughtfully*) It's a possibility, I suppose …

LUCY: (*Having made a decision*) Is the car outside?

CLIVE: Yes.

LUCY: I'll see you there in ten minutes.

CLIVE: (*Quietly, nodding*) All right, Lucy.

*LUCY goes out. CLIVE stands looking towards the door after her.*

LAURENCE: (*Still worried*) I don't like it, Clive. I think you're taking a risk.

CLIVE: (*Quietly, still looking towards the door, his thoughts on Lucy*) Yes, I think so, too – but we're going to take it.

CUT TO: A signpost which reads: Lower Meldon 3 Aylesbury 9. The signpost is on a deserted country road. It is afternoon.

*CLIVE's car appears and slows down at the signpost. LUCY looks out of the window at the signpost, then she turns and nods to CLIVE who is driving the car. The car continues down the road.*

CUT TO: *CLIVE's car is proceeding down a side road. GEORGE HARRIS, a farm labourer, can be seen in the distance cycling towards the car. The car slows down. The car stops with GEORGE slowly approaching on his bicycle. As he draws near the car, GEORGE gets off his bicycle and proceeds to push it past the Bentley. CLIVE winds down the window and speaks to him.*

CLIVE: Is this Lower Meldon?

GEORGE: No, sir, you've got another mile to go yet.

CLIVE: We're looking for Ashtree Cottage.

GEORGE: Oh, that's Mr Nelson's place. You turn left about half a mile up the road.

CLIVE: About half a mile?

GEORGE: That's right. Pigback Lane. You'll have a job getting the car down, sir.

CLIVE: How far down is the cottage?

GEORGE: Oh, about fifty yards, maybe a bit more. Stands well back on the left-hand side. If I was you, I'd leave the car at the top of the lane and walk down.

CLIVE: Thanks for the tip. (*Pleasantly*) Do you happen to know Mr Nelson?

GEORGE: I've seen him about, but he only comes down at weekends.

LUCY: (*Leaning forward to speak to GEORGE*) Is there a Mrs Nelson do you know?

GEORGE: Well, happen there must be, ma'am, since he's got a daughter, but I haven't seen her.

CLIVE: How do you know he's got a daughter?

GEORGE: He brought 'er down 'ere about ten days ago. Didn't see a lot of 'er.

CLIVE: (*Unable to conceal the tenseness in his voice*) How old?

GEORGE: What d'yer mean – how old?

CLIVE: How old was his daughter?

*GEORGE takes off his cap and scratches his head.*

GEORGE: Oh, I dunno. Now you're askin' … ten, twelve, perhaps … I dunno.

*CLIVE is about to change gear.*

CLIVE: Half a mile down the road, you said – on the left-hand side?

GEORGE: That's right. Pigback Lane. You can't miss it.

CLIVE: (*With a friendly nod*) Thank you very much.

GEORGE: You're welcome.

*CLIVE changes gear, lets in the clutch and the car moves forward. GEORGE stands watching it for a moment, then he turns and gets on his bicycle.*


CUT TO: Exterior of Ashtree Cottage, which is a farm labourer's cottage in an isolated dell. A path leads from a stile down to the Cottage.

*CLIVE is standing at the front door of the cottage. He knocks on the door but receives no reply. After a moment, he knocks again, but there is still no response. He stands back from the door, surveying the cottage, then he walks round to the side of the building. He peers through a small side window, then strolls round to the rear of the building.*

CUT TO: The front of the cottage.

*CLIVE returns from the rear of the cottage and crosses again towards the front door. He peers through the letterbox, then turns and strolls in the direction of the stile.*

CUT TO: *CLIVE reaches the stile at the same time as LUCY who approaches it from the country lane on the opposite side.*

CLIVE: The cottage is empty …

LUCY: Are you sure?

CLIVE: Yes …

LUCY: It looks a pretty derelict sort of place.

CLIVE: I don't think it's been used a great deal. I went round the back and looked through one of the windows.

*CLIVE stops speaking, staring down into the ditch by the stile. LUCY looks at him, obviously surprised, then follows his gaze. A small dark object – a schoolgirl's beret – is hanging on the long grass. CLIVE picks it up.*

LUCY: It's Janet's!

*LUCY takes the beret out of CLIVE's hand.*

CLIVE: Yes … (*Quietly, yet quickly*) Lucy, go back to the car and wait for me. If I'm not there in fifteen minutes fetch the police.

LUCY: What are you going to do?

CLIVE: (*Tensely*) Do as I say, Lucy … Give me fifteen minutes, then fetch the police!

*CLIVE quickly turns and walks back towards the cottage.*

CUT TO: The Living room of Ashtree Cottage.

This is a typical country-cottage-style room. There is a dilapidated settee with a chair to match, also a wing-back chair which faces the back window and stands near a small writing desk. There is a radio set, telephone, bottles,

119

glasses and syphon on a side table. A door to the left leads to the staircase and the bedrooms. A second door to the right to the kitchen.

*From the kitchen there is the sound of glass breaking, a stool being overturned and a muttered oath from CLIVE. He enters from the kitchen wrapping a handkerchief round his left hand, having obviously scratched it. He passes in front of the settee, looks round the room and then goes out the door on the left to search the rest of the cottage. After a little while he returns, again looks round the room and then crosses to the writing desk. He opens the desk and is about to examine the contents when suddenly, with a quick tense movement, he senses that someone is sitting in the wing-chair. He quickly turns and sees RUTH CALTHORPE sitting in the chair. Her eyes are closed, and she is motionless. CLIVE puts out his hand and touches her shoulder. Suddenly she falls forward, her head dropping to one side.*

CUT TO:  CLIVE's Bentley is parked at the junction of the road and the country lane.
*LUCY is walking up and down by the side of the car, obviously restless and worried. She still holds the beret in her hand and frequently consults her watch.*

CUT TO:  The Living room of Ashtree Cottage.
*CLIVE is standing by the telephone, holding the receiver, looking down at the body of RUTH CALTHORPE. He looks tense and nervous. There is a number ringing out on the telephone. After a moment, the receiver is lifted at the other end.*

WAINWRIGHT: Meldon Police Station, Sergeant Wainwright speaking.

CLIVE: Send someone to Ashtree Cottage, immediately!

WAINWRIGHT: Who is speaking, please?

CLIVE: (*Tensely*) Did you hear what I said? Send someone to Ashtree Cottage, Lower Meldon, straight away – it's very urgent … (*He replaces the receiver*)

CUT TO: *LUCY is sitting in the driving seat of the Bentley, waiting for CLIVE who suddenly appears, running towards the car from the country lane. As soon as he reaches the car he opens the door and climbs inside.*

LUCY: What's happened?

CLIVE: (*Shaking his head, tensely*) There's no sign of Janet. Get back onto the main road.

LUCY: Clive, you've cut your hand!

CLIVE: It's nothing …

LUCY: (*Suspiciously*) What's happened?

CLIVE: (*Urgently*) I'll tell you later, Lucy. Start the car and get back on the main road!

*LUCY looks at him, down at the handkerchief on his hand, then starts the car.*

CUT TO: *The car racing past the signpost to Lower Meldon.*

CUT TO: *The interior of the car as it travels along the main road, LUCY at the driving wheel.*

LUCY: (*Quietly*) How long has she been there?

CLIVE: I don't know …

LUCY: Did you examine her?

CLIVE: Only briefly, only to make sure she was dead.

LUCY: (*After a moment*) How did she die, do you know?

CLIVE: There was no sign of violence, but … (*He hesitates and LUCY looks at him*) … I think she was poisoned …

*As CLIVE speaks, a police car races past and he quickly turns his head and looks through the rear window.*

CLIVE: That's the police!


CUT TO: The Drawing room at Amberley. Later the same day.

*CLIVE enters, carrying the beret. He sits down on the arm of the settee, thoughtfully looks at the beret, then takes out his cigarette case and lights a cigarette. He is looking at the beret again, deep in thought, when LUCY enters from the hall, carrying a tea tray with tea things on it.*

LUCY: I've made some tea, Clive.

CLIVE: Where's Anna?

LUCY: She's out. I think she must have gone into the village. (*She sits down, arranges the tray on the table and pours the tea*) Would you like a cup?

CLIVE: No. No, I'm going to have a whiskey and soda. (*He puts down the beret, crosses to the drinks table and mixes himself the whiskey and soda*)

LUCY: (*Quietly*) Clive …

CLIVE: (*Turning*) Yes?

LUCY: (*Indicating the beret*) What do you think this means?

CLIVE: I don't know. I've been thinking about it. (*He moves towards LUCY*) I can't really find a satisfactory explanation. (*He sits on the arm of the settee*) You see, if Janet was at the cottage and they suddenly decided to take her away …

122

|        |                                                                                 |
|--------|---------------------------------------------------------------------------------|
|        | (*Changes his mind, shakes his head*) No … it just doesn't make sense …         |
| LUCY:  | What were you going to say?                                                      |
| CLIVE: | I was going to say if she resisted – started fighting – the beret might have fallen off her head. |
| LUCY:  | That's what I thought.                                                           |
| CLIVE: | But it doesn't add up, Lucy. She's only a child. Besides, they'd have noticed it … |
| LUCY:  | I'm not sure. It was in a ditch, remember.                                       |
| CLIVE: | We noticed it …                                                                  |
| LUCY:  | Yes, I know but … (*She stops, obviously having thought of something*)          |
| CLIVE: | (*Looking at her*) Go on …                                                       |

*LUCY rises, turns, and looks at CLIVE.*

|        |                                                                                 |
|--------|---------------------------------------------------------------------------------|
| LUCY:  | Clive, you don't think you were meant to find the beret? You don't think it was put there deliberately? |
| CLIVE: | But why should they do that?                                                     |
| LUCY:  | It was after you found it that you broke into the cottage.                       |
| CLIVE: | Well?                                                                            |
| LUCY:  | Well, they must have known that would be your reaction. Perhaps they wanted you to go into the cottage – perhaps they wanted you to find Miss Calthorpe. |
| CLIVE: | (*Puzzled*) But no one knew we were going down there …                           |
| LUCY:  | Laurence knew …                                                                  |
| CLIVE: | Yes, but Laurence is in Oxford. Besides, he wouldn't say … (*He stops*)          |
| LUCY:  | What are you thinking?                                                           |
| CLIVE: | (*Thoughtfully*) I wonder if I've been stupid about this? I wonder if that fellow Stevens |

knew I was going to search the file? He went out of the room while I was there – I wonder if that was done deliberately?

*There is a pause.*

*LUCY looks at CLIVE as he stands considering this point.*

*After a moment she moves towards him.*

LUCY: (*Quietly*) Clive, I want to ask you something. Please tell me the truth – tell me what you really think?

CLIVE: Well?

LUCY: Do you think Janet's – all right?

*CLIVE hesitates for a moment before replying.*

CLIVE: I don't know. If it hadn't been for that telephone call of yours I ... well, I should have had my doubts. But you spoke to her. You said you were sure that it was Janet.

LUCY: Yes, it was Janet all right. It was her voice. I recognised it at once. But ... that was several days ago. A lot might have happened since then.

CLIVE: (*Nodding*) A lot has happened.

LUCY: Clive, I know I'm going back on what I said this morning – but I think you'd better go to the Inspector, you'd better tell him the whole story ...

CLIVE: Is that what you want?

LUCY: Yes ...

CLIVE: (*Quietly*) I'll do whatever you want me to do, Lucy. If you'd rather I didn't speak to Kenton ...

LUCY: No. No, I don't think that's fair. I know we've Janet to think of, she's our first consideration but ...

CLIVE: She's our only consideration, Lucy.

LUCY:       (*Obviously worried, shaking her head*) No …
            I'm worried about you, Clive – about what
            happened to Nelson. About this afternoon …
CLIVE:      This afternoon?
LUCY:       Supposing the police find out that you went to
            the cottage – supposing they think you had an
            appointment with Miss Calthorpe?
CLIVE:      But why should they think that?
LUCY:       I don't know why, but supposing they do?
CLIVE:      You think they might jump to the conclusion
            that I murdered her?

*LUCY nods. CLIVE looks thoughtful. He stubs out his
cigarette in the ashtray on the table.*

CLIVE:      (*Turning*) If I talk to Kenton, I've got to tell
            him the whole story. You realise that?
LUCY:       Yes.
CLIVE:      I've got to tell him about you and Pelford and
            the telephone call …
LUCY:       Yes, of course. (*Moving towards CLIVE*)
            Clive, I think you've got to do it.

*CLIVE looks at LUCY and hesitates.*

LUCY:       After all, if we don't consult Kenton what do
            we do? We can't find Pelford. We've tried …

*CLIVE nods and turns away from the table.*

CLIVE:      I wish to God we could find Pelford. In my
            opinion he's the key to the whole situation …
LUCY:       Yes, but we've tried, darling. Isn't that why we
            went to the cottage in the first place?
CLIVE:      Yes. (*He looks at LUCY for a moment, then
            nods*) All right, Lucy – I'll phone Kenton.

*CLIVE crosses to the telephone on the desk and picks up
the receiver. He dials a number and stands waiting while
the number rings out. Suddenly he notices a small writing*

125

*pad on the desk. He picks it up, glances at it, then quickly replaces the telephone receiver.*

LUCY:     (*Surprised*) What is it, Clive? What's the matter?

*CLIVE moves towards LUCY still looking at the scribbling pad.*

CLIVE:    This is a note from Anna. She must have written it before she went out.

LUCY:     Well – what is it?

CLIVE:    (*Reading the note*) A Mr Pelford called – he said he'd telephone later …

LUCY:     Pelford?

CLIVE:    He must have telephoned this morning after we left.

LUCY:     I wonder if he left any message?

CLIVE:    It doesn't look like it.

*ANNA appears from the hall. She is wearing a hat and coat.*

ANNA:     May I come in, Mrs Freeman?

LUCY:     (*Turning*) Oh yes, come in, Anna!

ANNA:     I'm sorry I was out when you got back, I had to go into the village.

LUCY:     That's all right.

CLIVE:    (*Crossing to ANNA*) Anna, I've just found your note. What time did Mr Pelford call?

ANNA:     Mr Pelford? (*Remembering*) Oh, just after you left – about eleven o'clock.

CLIVE:    He didn't leave any message?

ANNA:     No – except that he would telephone later. (*Smiling*) He's a nice man. So polite. He shook hands when he arrived and when he left.

CLIVE:    Anna, what do you mean, when he arrived?

LUCY:     Do you mean he called here?

ANNA: Yes, but of course. (*To CLIVE*) Isn't that what I put in the note? Mr Pelford called …

CLIVE: Yes, but we thought you meant telephoned …

ANNA: No, no, I put telephone if I mean telephone …

CLIVE: This is important, Anna – very important. What did Mr Pelford say?

LUCY: Tell us exactly what happened.

ANNA: Well, he called just after you left and said he wanted to see you. When he realised I was Austrian he spoke German to me and naturally I understood every word he …

CLIVE: Yes, yes, Anna – but what did he say?

ANNA: He said you were a friend of his and that you were expecting him. He asked me if he could wait a little while. I didn't know how long you were going to be. You didn't say you were going to be out all day, Mrs Freeman, so naturally …

LUCY: No, no of course not. Go on, Anna …

ANNA: Well, he waited about half an hour and then he left.

CLIVE: Where did he wait – in here?

ANNA: Yes. (*Perturbed*) I hope I did the right thing, Mr Freeman – he seemed a very nice man.

CLIVE: Yes. Yes, that's all right, Anna.

*The telephone starts to ring.*

CLIVE: Now tell me, did he mention … (*He stops, turns and looks at the telephone*)

*LUCY looks at CLIVE. Then crosses and picks up the receiver.*

LUCY:          (*On phone*) Hello? Beacherscross 189.

PELFORD:    (*On the other end*) Mrs Freeman?

LUCY:          Yes.

PELFORD:    This is Mr Pelford. Could I speak to your husband, please?

LUCY:          (*Tensely*) One moment. (*She puts her hand over the receiver nods to CLIVE, hesitates, then puts the receiver down on the desk and crosses to ANNA. To ANNA*) Thank you, Anna, you can go.

*ANNA hesitates, assumes it is PELFORD on the telephone and goes out. CLIVE looks at LUCY, then crosses and picks up the receiver. LUCY moves closer to him.*

CLIVE:         (*On phone*) Hello?

PELFORD:    (*Pleasantly*) Mr Freeman?

CLIVE:         Yes.

PELFORD:    This is Pelford. I'm sorry I missed you this morning. It was most unfortunate.

CLIVE:         (*Deliberately angry*) Pelford, I've been trying to get in touch with you! I thought you said someone was coming to see me the other night?

PELFORD:    (*Politely surprised*) Didn't someone come and see you, Mr Freeman?

CLIVE:         No, they didn't!

PELFORD:    How very odd.

CLIVE:         Now, Pelford, listen to me …

PELFORD:    (*Interrupting him, quietly*) I think it would be more satisfactory if you listened to me, Mr Freeman. However, if you insist …

CLIVE:         (*After a moment*) What is it you want?

PELFORD:    I want to see you …

CLIVE:     When?

PELFORD:   This evening …

CLIVE:     All right, I shall be here. I suggest you call at nine o'clock.

PELFORD:   Nine o'clock isn't convenient.

CLIVE:     Well, when would you like to call?

PELFORD:   (*Quietly, yet taking control of the conversation*) Mr Freeman, do you know the main London-Birmingham road?

CLIVE:     Yes.

PELFORD:   Just south of Dunstable there's a pull-in for lorry drivers. It's called Eddie's. Eddie's for Eats. I'll see you there at eight o'clock.

CLIVE:     Do we have to meet at a place like that? Surely …

PELFORD:   Eight o'clock, Mr Freeman.

CLIVE:     (*Pause, then quietly*) All right.

PELFORD:   Oh, and by the way, I took the liberty of borrowing something this morning. I hope Mrs Freeman doesn't mind. I'll return it to you this evening.

CLIVE:     (*Puzzled*) What are you talking about. What did you borrow?

PELFORD:   (*Rather precise in manner*) A little woolly dog. Eight o'clock, Mr Freeman. Don't forget – Eddie's for Eats. (*He replaces the receiver*)

*CLIVE replaces the receiver and turns towards LUCY. He is obviously puzzled.*

LUCY:      What were you talking about, Clive?

CLIVE:     Lucy, has Janet got a small woolly dog?

LUCY:      Why yes – you remember you bought it for her in Switzerland the year before last.

129

CLIVE:       Where is it?
LUCY:        It's on the mantlepiece in the nursery. She always keeps it there.
CLIVE:       See if it's still there, Lucy.

*LUCY looks at CLIVE, then turns and goes out of the room. CLIVE takes out his cigarette case and lights a cigarette. He looks thoughtful and puzzled. He sits on the arm of the settee, smoking the cigarette. After a little while LUCY returns.*

CLIVE:   Well?
LUCY:    (*Surprised*) It's gone ...
CLIVE:   Was it there last night?
LUCY:    It was there this morning. I saw it before we went out.
CLIVE:   (*Nodding*) Pelford took it.
LUCY:    (*Puzzled*) Why?

*CLIVE doesn't reply. He sits deep in thought smoking his cigarette.*

LUCY:    Clive, why did Pelford take the dog?

*CLIVE turns and looks up at LUCY.*

CLIVE:   Don't you know why, Lucy?
LUCY:    (*Puzzled, shaking her head*) No ...
CLIVE:   (*Quietly*) He wanted to photograph it.

*LUCY looks at CLIVE, obviously a little bewildered.*


CUT TO: Eddie's For Eats Café, a pull-in for lorry drivers on the main London-Birmingham road. We see the café through the windscreen of PELFORD's car which is parked on the opposite side of the road.

*PELFORD is sitting in the car alone, watching the café. CLIVE's Bentley is parked on the parking lot outside the café.*

CUT TO: Inside Eddie's Café. Night.

The bar runs the length of the café. Wooden tables face the bar, benches by the tables.

*The café is deserted except for CLIVE, who sits at a corner table. EDDIE, a heavy-looking man in his late forties is taking CLIVE a cup of coffee.*

EDDIE:      You'd better 'ave a cuppa coffee, mate.

CLIVE:      Oh, thanks.

EDDIE:      It doesn't look as if this chum of yours is going to turn up.

CLIVE:      He said eight o'clock.

EDDIE:      It's nearly a quarter past nine. If you ask me you've 'ad it.

CLIVE:      What time do you close?

EDDIE:      We don't close, chum – we're open all night.

CLIVE:      I'll give him another half an hour.

EDDIE:      Okay. Would you like anything to eat?

CLIVE:      No, I don't think so, thanks. (*He takes out some silver and puts it on the table*) Keep the change.

EDDIE:      (*Picking up the silver*) Oh. Oh, ta. (*He leaves the table and goes back to the bar*)

*CLIVE looks down at the cup of coffee, lifts it and drinks. As he replaces the cup, a man's hand appears and puts a small woolly dog by the side of the saucer. CLIVE looks up and sees PELFORD who is wearing a dark mackintosh and a trilby hat.*

PELFORD:   Good evening.

CLIVE:      You said eight o'clock.

PELFORD:   I know. (*He sits down at the table*) I've been watching the café. I wanted to make certain you were alone. We don't want a

131

repetition of the Nelson affair, Mr Freeman.

*EDDIE arrives at the table.*

CLIVE: What do you mean? I don't know what you're talking about?

EDDIE: (*To PELFORD*) Coffee?

PELFORD: (*To EDDIE*) Is it possible to have a pot of tea?

EDDIE: (*Reluctantly*) Well, I can make you a pot if you feel like a pot of tea.

PELFORD: I do.

*EDDIE looks at him and goes back to the bar.*

CLIVE: What do you mean? Who's Nelson?

PELFORD: Who's Nelson? What an extraordinary memory you have, my friend. He's the man you murdered. The man you took to Henshaw Wood. But don't let's worry about Nelson. There are so many other things to talk about.

CLIVE: What – for instance?

*PELFORD touches the woolly dog and smiles at CLIVE.*

PELFORD: Your daughter.

CLIVE: (*Tensely*) Where is Janet?

PELFORD: Where she is at the moment is of little importance – it's where she'll be this time tomorrow that matters.

CLIVE: What do you mean? What are you going to do with her?

PELFORD: We intend handing her over to Mrs Freeman tomorrow afternoon at four o'clock. If it's convenient, of course.

CLIVE: Look, Pelford. I want my daughter back. I'll do anything within reason to get her back. Now what the hell is it you want?

PELFORD:    I'll tell you. But first of all – just in case you have a suspicious mind – I'd like to prove something to you. (*He takes a snapshot photograph out of his inside pocket*) I'd like to prove that we still have your daughter and that she's alive and quite well. (*He hands the snapshot to CLIVE*)

*CLIVE looks at the photograph which shows JANET standing against a garden wall clutching the small woolly dog. CLIVE looks up at PELFORD.*

PELFORD:    In case there's a doubt as to when the photograph was taken, I took it this afternoon. (*He leans over the table and points to the woolly dog in the photograph*) You'll observe she's holding the dog, so it couldn't possibly have been taken before …

CLIVE:    I get the point, Mr Pelford.

PEFORD:    Good. It's so much pleasanter when people see what you're getting at. You may keep the photograph. It's rather a nice one, I think; although we had a little difficulty in getting her to smile.

CLIVE:    (*Quietly, controlling himself*) What is it you want?

*There is a slight pause. PELFORD looks across at CLIVE.*

PELFORD:    Have you a passport?

CLIVE:    Why, yes.

PELFORD:    We want you to fly to Hamburg tomorrow afternoon. The plane leaves London airport at four o'clock.

CLIVE:    (*Surprised*) Hamburg?

PELFORD:    Yes.

133

CLIVE:      Why do you want me to go to Hamburg?

PELFORD:    You'll be told why – when you get there.

CLIVE:      But you can't expect me to get on a plane and go to Germany without knowing …

*PELFORD leans forward across the table and interrupts him.*

PELFORD:    Mr Freeman, before you get excited and reject the suggestion, let's clarify the situation. We're   simply asking you to fly to Hamburg, at our expense. (*Smiling*) We're not asking you to make the first trip to the moon. When you get to Hamburg, you'll be met by someone who will tell you exactly what it is we want you to do.

CLIVE:      And supposing I don't want to do it?

PELFORD:    That would be – unfortunate, to say the least.

CLIVE:      Unfortunate for whom – my daughter?

*EDDIE arrives at the table with a pot of tea.*

PELFORD:    For everyone concerned. (*As he pours himself a cup of tea*) Would you care for another coffee?

CLIVE:      No.

*EDDIE looks at CLIVE then returns to the bar.*

CLIVE:      (*Leaning across the table*) Now, Pelford, listen. I'm not a poor man. In fact, I'm pretty well off …

PELFORD:    (*With emphasis, stirring his tea, almost a shade petulant*) It isn't a question of money …

CLIVE:      (*Angry*) Well, what is it a question of?

*PELFORD sips his tea, looks at CLIVE, puts down the cup, takes a handkerchief from his sleeve and pats his lips.*

PELFORD: You've reached a time of day, Mr Freeman. A time of day when you've got to make a decision. Let me put the proposition to you, quite simply. If you don't go to Hamburg tomorrow your daughter will not be returned, and you'll find yourself facing a murder charge.

CLIVE: (*Angry*) A murder charge? What are you talking about? I didn't murder Nelson! The worst that can happen is that ...

PELFORD: (*Stopping him*) Wait a moment, please! On the other hand, if you do go to Hamburg, I give you my word of honour that the moment you step into that plane Janet will be ...

CLIVE: Your word of honour? Good God, man, do you think I'm crazy?

PELFORD: (*Quietly*) Mr Freeman, there's no necessity to be rude. If you don't wish to pursue the conversation just say so. (*A pause*) You know we've got to trust each other – if we don't trust each other we'll get precisely nowhere. The moment you step into the plane Janet will be released and handed over to your wife. I assure you, there's no doubt about that – not a flicker of doubt. It's you we're interested in, Mr Freeman, not your little girl – charming though she is.

CLIVE: And if I don't go to Hamburg?

PELFORD: I've told you what will happen if you don't go; but for goodness sake don't let's even consider that contingency. It's far too unpleasant. (*Leans forward across*

135

*the table*) My dear fellow, you've got to go, for your own sake as well as Janet's.

CLIVE: (*Looking straight at PELFORD*) I want to know more about this. How long do I stay in Hamburg? Who meets me? What is it you want me to do?

PELFORD: You'll stay in Hamburg approximately twenty-four hours. You'll be met be an Englishman who will take you to a house on the outskirts of the city. (*A moment, watching CLIVE*) The following afternoon you'll leave for Prague.

CLIVE: (*Surprised*) Prague?

PELFORD: Yes.

CLIVE: And how long do I stay in Prague?

PELFORD: That depends, Mr Freeman …

CLIVE: On what?

PELFORD: On a number of things; but I should be prepared for a lengthy stay if I were you. (*Looks at his watch*) It's just half past nine. We want your decision by twelve o'clock tomorrow afternoon. You've got just fifteen hours.

CLIVE: And if I agree to do this?

PELFORD: Janet will be put on the three ten from Marylebone tomorrow afternoon. I suggest your wife meets the train at Beacherscross. (*Looks at CLIVE; with sincerity*) There'll be no nonsense, Mr Freeman. She'll be on that train, I assure you.

CLIVE: How shall I know that? How shall I know whether you've kept your word?

PELFORD:      You'll see the English newspapers before you leave Hamburg. (*A shrug*) Perhaps they'll allow you to telephone …

*A pause. PELFORD waits, watching CLIVE.*

CLIVE:        (*Quietly*) I want time to think about this …

PELFORD:      Very well. (*He picks up the photograph, takes out a pencil and scribbles a number on the back of it*) If you decide to do the right thing ring that number any time between midnight and twelve o'clock tomorrow morning. Just say, "I'd like the reservation".

CLIVE:        (*Picking up the telephone*) And then what?

PELFORD:      We shall expect you at London airport at two thirty tomorrow afternoon. (*He rises from the table*) Goodnight. (*He moves away and then with almost an afterthought turns back and looks at CLIVE*) Oh, and Mr Freeman, speaking purely from a personal point of view, don't think I don't appreciate your difficulties, because I do. But do try and be sensible about this. Goodnight.

*CLIVE doesn't look up as PELFORD walks away. He is deep in thought, playing with the small woolly dog.*

CUT TO:  The Drawing Room at Amberley.

It is late the same night.

*The clock in the hall is striking eleven. DETECTIVE INSPECTOR KENTON is standing looking towards the French windows, the curtains of which are drawn. He wears an overcoat and carries his hat. He turns as LUCY enters from the hall. She is wearing a dressing gown.*

137

KENTON:  Mrs Freeman, I'm sorry to disturb you at this hour of the night.

LUCY:  (*A shade nervous*) I'm afraid my husband's out, Inspector. He's gone up to Town. He won't be back until very late.

KENTON:  It wasn't your husband I wanted to see.

LUCY:  Oh. (*A moment*) Er – won't you sit down, Inspector?

KENTON: Thank you. (*He sits in the armchair*)

*LUCY sits on the settee, facing KENTON.*

*There is a slight pause.*

LUCY:  If it wasn't my husband you wanted to see, then obviously …

KENTON: (*Interrupting her, leaning forward slightly*) Mrs Freeman, I'd like to ask you one or two questions about your husband. If you'd prefer not to answer them, don't hesitate to say so. I shall quite understand.

LUCY:  Go on, Inspector.

KENTON: Well, perhaps I'd better begin by telling you about Miss Calthorpe. Miss Calthorpe's dead.

LUCY:  (*Nervously, apparently surprised*) Dead?

KENTON: Yes. Her body was found this afternoon in a cottage near Aylesbury.

LUCY:  How did she die?

KENTON: We're having an autopsy early tomorrow morning. But there seems to be very little doubt that she was poisoned.

LUCY:  You mean – she was murdered.

KENTON: Yes, Mrs Freeman – that's what I mean.

*KENTON watches LUCY for a moment and LUCY becomes faintly embarrassed, then suddenly KENTON takes an envelope out of his pocket and extracts a letter from the envelope.*

138

KENTON: Would you be kind enough to look at the writing on this envelope?

*LUCY takes the envelope and looks at it. The envelope is marked "Personal" and is addressed to Miss Ruth Calthorpe, Green Tiles Preparatory School, Beacherscross, Hertfordshire.*

*LUCY looks up at the INSPECTOR.*

KENTON: Do you recognise the handwriting?

LUCY:    (*Puzzled and surprised*) Why, yes – it's my husband's.

*KENTON nods and takes the envelope from LUCY.*

KENTON: (*Quietly*) Thank you. That's what I thought. Now I'll read you the letter, Mrs Freeman. (*He opens the letter, takes a pair of glasses from his breast pocket, puts them on and after a moment starts to read them*) "Dear Ruth ... I think it's imperative that we meet again, and I suggest that you go to the cottage on Saturday morning. I'll try and get there in the afternoon about three o'clock, although of course there may be difficulties. I'd like you to take Janet's beret and place it in the ditch near the stile, then if Lucy – or Laurence Hudson – insists on coming down I can discover the beret and use it as an excuse for entering the cottage. Yours, Clive."

*KENTON looks up. LUCY rises from the settee.*

LUCY:    (*Tensely*) Where did you find that letter?

KENTON: (*Watching LUCY, quietly*) It was in Miss Calthorpe's handbag.

# END OF EPISODE FOUR

# EPISODE FIVE

OPEN TO: The Drawing Room at Amberley.

*DETECTIVE INSPECTOR KENTON is facing LUCY, reading the letter.*

KENTON: (*Reading*) "Dear Ruth … I think it's imperative that we meet again, and I suggest that you go to the cottage on Saturday morning. I'll try and get there in the afternoon about three o'clock, although of course there may be difficulties. I'd like you to take Janet's beret and place it in the ditch near the stile, then if Lucy – or Laurence Hudson – insists on coming down I can discover the beret and use it as an excuse for entering the cottage. Yours, Clive."

*KENTON looks up. LUCY rises from the settee.*

LUCY:     (*Tensely*) Where did you find that letter?

KENTON: (*Watching LUCY, quietly*) It was in Miss Calthorpe's handbag. (*He hands LUCY the letter*)

LUCY:     (*Staring at the letter*) Clive didn't write this …

KENTON: Isn't it his handwriting?

LUCY:     Yes, it looks like it, but –

KENTON: Then what makes you think he didn't write it?

LUCY:     (*Bewildered*) He couldn't have done! It's … impossible!

KENTON: Why?

LUCY:     Well, for one thing, he hardly knew Miss Calthorpe.

KENTON: How do you know that?

LUCY:     Well – I just know, that's all.

KENTON: You mean you know everything about your husband? Who his friends are? What he does in his spare time?

LUCY:     (*Irritated*) No, I didn't say that.

KENTON: That's what you implied.

143

*LUCY is a shade surprised by KENTON's unmistakable change of manner. He is by no means as friendly as usual. KENTON takes the letter from her.*

KENTON: (*Suddenly taking everything for granted*) Did you find the beret?

LUCY: (*Playing for time: on guard*) The – what?

KENTON: (*Impatiently, tapping the letter*) The beret – did you find it?

LUCY: (*Apparently surprised*) Why no! Look, Inspector, my husband doesn't know anything about this business …

*KENTON looks at LUCY. He hesitates, then:*

KENTON: Mrs Freeman, where were you at half past three this afternoon?

LUCY: I was here.

KENTON: Alone?

LUCY: No, my husband was with me.

KENTON: Did someone borrow his car, then?

LUCY: What do you mean?

KENTON: (*Impatiently*) You know perfectly well what I mean. His car was seen this afternoon at Lower Meldon in Hertfordshire.

LUCY: (*Hesitant*) I don't see how it could have been.

KENTON: I can assure you it was. (*A moment, quietly*) Why don't you tell me the truth?

LUCY: (*A shade annoyed*) I am telling you the truth …

KENTON: (*Shaking his head*) I'm sorry, I don't believe you.

LUCY: Really, Inspector! I don't think you've any right to …

KENTON: (*Interrupting LUCY*) Mrs Freeman, I'm investigating a murder case. There are certain things I've got to find out. The whereabouts of you and your husband at three thirty this afternoon happens to be one of them.

LUCY: I've told you. We were both here this afternoon.

*KENTON sits on the arm of the settee, looks at LUCY and slowly shakes his head.*

KENTON: I'm sorry. I find that very difficult to believe.

*LUCY is about to retaliate but KENTON lifts his hand and stops her.*

KENTON: I have a theory about this afternoon, Mrs Freeman, and I'd like you to listen to it. I think your husband had an appointment with Miss Calthorpe. I think in some strange way they were both concerned with the disappearance of your daughter. I think …

*He stops speaking and turns towards the hall. LUCY also looks towards the door. After a moment CLIVE enters. He is still wearing his overcoat and is returning his keys to his pocket.*

CLIVE: (*Quietly, sensing that he has walked in at an awkward moment*) Hello, Inspector! I thought I recognised your voice.

LUCY: (*To CLIVE, quickly*) Miss Calthorpe's been murdered and the Inspector's trying to …

KENTON: (*Rising, annoyed*) One moment, Mrs Freeman, please!

CLIVE: (*To KENTON*) Miss Calthorpe – Janet's teacher?

KENTON: Mr Freeman, where were you this afternoon between one o'clock and a quarter past four?

LUCY: (*Interrupting him, angrily*) I told you where we were this afternoon! (*To CLIVE*) Clive, the Inspector simply refused to believe a word I say!

145

KENTON:(*Interrupting her*) Mrs Freeman, I must ask you not to …

CLIVE: (*To LUCY, stopping them both*) Darling, please! (*To KENTON, quite calmly*) Where was I between one o'clock and …?

KENTON: … A quarter past four.

CLIVE: I was here, Inspector. At home …

*KENTON looks at CLIVE, then at LUCY, then back at CLIVE again.*

KENTON:(*To CLIVE*) Miss Calthorpe's body was found in a cottage at a place called Lower Meldon – that's near Aylesbury. The local police were sent for and on the way to the cottage they passed a Bentley, registration number TXP367.

*CLIVE looks at the INSPECTOR, takes off his overcoat and puts it over the back of the settee.*

CLIVE: (*As he puts down the coat*) They made a mistake …

KENTON: What do you mean, sir?

CLIVE: I mean they made a mistake. They couldn't have passed a car with that registration number.

KENTON: Why not?

CLIVE: Because that happens to be my Bentley and it certainly wasn't anywhere near Aylesbury this afternoon.

*KENTON moves towards CLIVE.*

KENTON: I hope you know what you're saying, sir.

CLIVE: Of course I know what I'm saying. I'm saying my car wasn't anywhere near Aylesbury. And neither was I, Inspector.

KENTON: Mr Freeman, just before you arrived, I showed your wife a letter. I'd like you to read it.

*KENTON takes the letter out of his pocket and hands it to CLIVE. CLIVE looks at the INSPECTOR, glances across at LUCY, then starts to read. After he has finished reading the letter CLIVE looks up and across at LUCY who is watching him.*

KENTON: Well, sir?

CLIVE: (*Turning to the Inspector*) Where did you get this?

KENTON: It was in Miss Calthorpe's handbag.

CLIVE: I see. So you think I went to Lower Meldon this afternoon because I had an appointment with Miss Calthorpe?

KENTON: Wouldn't you think that if you were in my shoes and you read that letter?

CLIVE: If I were in your shoes, I'd make certain the letter was genuine before I accused …

KENTON: (*Interrupting him*) It is genuine, sir.

CLIVE: I'm sorry to disappoint you.

LUCY: (*To CLIVE*) You mean you didn't write it?

CLIVE: Of course I didn't write it!

KENTON: It's your handwriting.

CLIVE: It's a copy of my handwriting and a very good copy. (*Shaking his head, handing the letter back to KENTON*) But I didn't write it.

KENTON: Mr Freeman, I don't think you appreciate the seriousness of the situation …

CLIVE: I can assure you I do, Inspector.

KENTON: If, in spite of what you say, this letter turns out to be genuine – and it's established that you were in Lower Meldon this afternoon – then in my opinion it won't be long before you'll find yourself facing a murder charge.

CLIVE: (*Quite pleasantly*) Ought you to say that, Inspector, without first warning me that anything I say …

147

KENTON: (*Interrupting him*) I'm just giving you my opinion, sir – it's strictly off the record. I don't want either you or Mrs Freeman to be under any delusions.

CLIVE: Inspector, let's assume for the moment that that letter is genuine, that I did in fact have an appointment with Miss Calthorpe.

KENTON: Yes, sir?

CLIVE: The assumption, surely would be that my appointment was of a strictly personal nature. The letter implies that.

KENTON: (*Interested, nodding*) Yes …

CLIVE: Well, in that case, why should I take my wife with me?

KENTON: (*Quietly, watching him*) Did you take Mrs Freeman with you?

CLIVE: No, but … (*Hesitates, realising he may have made a slip*)

KENTON: (*Politely*) Go on, sir.

CLIVE: You've been questioning my wife. You've assumed that we were both at Lower Meldon this afternoon.

KENTON: My assumption was based on the fact that two people were seen – a man and a woman – in a Bentley – TXP367. That's your registration number.

CLIVE: Yes, I know, but –

KENTON: (*Stopping him, closing the interview*) Mr Freeman, I wouldn't say any more just as the moment if I were you. Have a word with Mr Hudson.

CLIVE: (*Irritated*) What's Laurence got to do with it?

KENTON: He's your lawyer, isn't he, sir?

CLIVE: Yes.

KENTON: Well, have a talk with Mr Hudson, and give me a ring tomorrow morning. The earlier the better, sir. (*To LUCY*) Goodnight, Mrs Freeman.

LUCY: Goodnight.

KENTON: (*To CLIVE*) It's all right, I can see myself out.

*KENTON crosses to the door, then stops and turns towards CLIVE who is standing watching him.*

KENTON: Oh, there's just one point. You might care to make a note of it. When you tell Mr Hudson about the letter …

CLIVE: Yes?

KENTON: Don't forget to tell him it was in Miss Calthorpe's handbag. The handbag was by the side of the chair.

LUCY: (*Looking at Kenton, puzzled*) Is that important?

KENTON: (*With the first suggestion of a smile*) If I was your husband I should consider it important, Mrs Freeman. (*Looking at CLIVE*) Goodnight, sir.

*KENTON goes out. Both CLIVE and LUCY stand motionless, looking towards the hall, waiting for the sound of the front door closing. LUCY turns towards CLIVE as the sound of the front door is heard off.*

LUCY: Clive, what did he mean – about the handbag?

CLIVE: (*Thoughtfully*) I don't know.

*LUCY moves towards CLIVE.*

LUCY: (*Quietly, facing him*) Did you write that letter?

CLIVE: (*Surprised*) Why, no …

LUCY: Had you an appointment with Miss Calthorpe?

CLIVE: Of course not! (*Taking hold of LUCY's arm*) Lucy, you don't think …

LUCY:       (*Interrupting him*) It was your handwriting. It mentioned the beret. It was you that first pointed out …

CLIVE:      (*Interrupting LUCY*) It wasn't my handwriting! (*Pulling her towards him*) Good God, Lucy, if you don't believe me how can we expect Kenton to?

LUCY:       (*Releasing herself, looking at CLIVE tensely*) Clive, I don't know what's behind all this, I don't know whether you were friendly with Ruth Calthorpe or not. I don't honestly care. The only thing I'm interested in …

CLIVE:      (*Angry*) Lucy, for goodness sake! You know why we went to that cottage – because we thought Janet might be there! It was your idea that we went to Lower Meldon, not mine! I wanted to tell the Inspector the whole story, but you wouldn't let me.

LUCY:       (*Looking at CLIVE, quietly surprised*) It was you that suggested going down to the cottage.

CLIVE:      (*Shaking his head*) It wasn't, Lucy.

LUCY:       Clive, after you came back from Stevens' place you said …

CLIVE:      (*Angrily*) Well, what the hell does it matter who suggested it? (*He grabs hold of LUCY's arm again*) I hadn't an appointment with Ruth Calthorpe and I didn't write that letter! You've got to believe that, Lucy.

LUCY:       Then who did write it?

CLIVE:      I don't know …

*LUCY breaks away and crosses to the drinks table. She stands with her back to CLIVE. After a moment*:

CLIVE:      You don't believe me, do you? You think I'm lying?

LUCY:      (*Emotionally; near to tears*) I just don't know
           what to believe. (*A moment*) Did you see
           Pelford? What happened tonight?

*There is a long pause. CLIVE stands looking at LUCY.*

CLIVE:     (*Quietly*) Janet's coming home …

*LUCY swings round and faces CLIVE.*

CLIVE:     They're putting her on the three-ten from
           Marylebone tomorrow afternoon. They want
           you to meet the train at Beacherscross.

LUCY:      (*Slowly, moving towards CLIVE*) Clive … is
           this true?

CLIVE:     (*Nodding*) Yes … (*Hesitant*) I'm going up to
           Town tomorrow to see Pelford.

LUCY:      But what happened? Tell me what happened!

*CLIVE looks at LUCY, hesitates, then as he speaks half
turns away from her.*

CLIVE:     Pelford didn't turn up. I think he was
           frightened. I waited an hour then he telephoned
           me. He wants five thousand pounds … I've
           promised to hand the money over tomorrow
           afternoon.

LUCY:      But when I saw him, he said it wasn't a
           question of money.

CLIVE:     (*A note of tenseness in his voice*) It's always a
           question of money, Lucy – in the end …

LUCY:      You think he means it? You don't think he'll
           change his mind?

CLIVE:     He means it all right. He's scared. Besides, I
           think they've had enough of this business, they
           want to release Janet … (*He turns and touches
           LUCY's arm*) She'll be here tomorrow – I
           promise you.

*LUCY is stunned by the news.*

*After a moment LUCY turns away from CLIVE and starts to cry. CLIVE watches her and then quietly goes out of the room.*

*After a little while LUCY stops crying, uses her handkerchief and crosses to the drinks table. She picks up a cigarette and a lighter. Her hand is unsteady and the lighter refuses to work. She tries it several times, then notices CLIVE's overcoat on the settee. She puts down the lighter, crosses to the settee and feels in the pockets of the overcoat. She produces a box of matches and at the same time takes out the snapshot photograph. She stares at the snapshot in amazement. She turns it over and notices the scribbled telephone number on the back of it. Suddenly the telephone bell gives a little tinkle and LUCY turns, stares across at the desk, then up towards the room above. It is obvious what she is thinking – CLIVE is telephoning from the bedroom. LUCY crosses to the desk, hesitates, then gently lifts the receiver and listens. A number is ringing out, but there appears to be no reply. For a little while we hear the ringing out tone, then suddenly the receiver is lifted, and a man's voice can be heard.*

MAN:      (*On the other end*) Drake Hotel …

CLIVE:    (*Voice*) Is that Bayswater 8621?

MAN:      Yes … Drake Hotel …

CLIVE:    My name is Freeman. I have a message for Mr Pelford.

MAN:      Oh, yes.  What is it?

CLIVE:    (*After a momentary hesitation*) Tell him I'll take the reservation.

MAN:      All right, Mr Freeman. I'll see he gets the message. Thanks for ringing.

*The receiver is replaced, and the dialling tone starts; CLIVE replaces his receiver in the bedroom. LUCY slowly puts down the phone and turns away from the table. She is puzzled and obviously worried. She moves onto the settee again, still looking at the snapshot. After a moment she picks up CLIVE's overcoat and replaces the snapshot and the box of matches.*

CUT TO:   The Drawing Room at Amberley.   Afternoon.
*CLIVE enters, carrying his hat and suitcase, his overcoat over his arm. He puts the suitcase down on the settee and places the overcoat over the back of a chair. He turns, crosses to a picture on the far wall. The picture conceals a small built-in wall safe. He swings the picture away from the wall, unlocks the safe, and extracts several documents, and a passport. He looks at the documents, replaces them in the safe, and puts his passport in his pocket. After moving the picture back into position again he turns to the settee, suddenly his eye catches a framed photograph of LUCY and JANET. He crosses to the table on which the photograph stands; looks down at the photograph for a moment, then picks it up and crosses to the settee. He puts the photograph in the suitcase and is locking the case when LUCY enters from the hall.*

LUCY:     There's a taxi outside; did you send for it?
CLIVE:    Yes. (*Hesitant*) I'm catching the two o'clock train.
LUCY:     What time will you be back?
CLIVE:    (*Not looking at her*) Sometime this evening. I'll phone you.
LUCY:     (*Indicating the suitcase*) Supposing they don't keep their word? Supposing Janet isn't on the train?
CLIVE:    That's a risk we've got to take. But she'll be on that train, Lucy, I'm sure. (*He looks at LUCY*) Four o'clock – Beacherscross.

LUCY:      (*Nodding, watching him*) I'll be there long
           before four o'clock, Clive. (*A moment*) Where
           are you seeing Pelford?
CLIVE:     (*Hesitant*) At the studio.
LUCY:      You've got the money, then?
CLIVE:     (*Nodding towards the suitcase*) Yes.
LUCY:      When did you get it?
CLIVE:     (*Surprised by the question*) Why, this morning.
           You saw me go out. I told you I was going to
           the bank.
LUCY:      (*Quietly*) Yes, but you didn't go.

*CLIVE looks at her.*

LUCY:      I spoke to Talbotson, the manager ... he said
           you hadn't been in.
CLIVE:     He's mistaken. I went in just after ...
LUCY:      (*Interrupting him, shaking her head*) You
           didn't. Clive. Talbotson wasn't mistaken ...
           you haven't been near the bank.

*A moment.*

LUCY:      What happened last night?
CLIVE:     (*Tensely*) I've told you what happened!
LUCY:      (*Shaking her head*) You saw Pelford. He made
           you a proposition and you accepted it.
CLIVE:     (*A shade hurt*) I've told you what happened.
           He wants five thousand pounds ...
LUCY:      I don't believe that story! (*Taking hold of
           CLIVE's arm, tensely*) Clive, I want to know
           what happened?
CLIVE:     (*A moment, looking at LUCY*) What happened
           last night  is  completely  unimportant.
           (*Releasing himself*) Goodbye ... Give Janet my
           love ...
LUCY:      (*Tensely, moving back from CLIVE*) If you
           don't tell me what happened I'll phone the

|        | Inspector! I'll tell him the whole story. I'll tell him you saw Pelford and that … |
|--------|-----|
| CLIVE: | (*Quietly, interrupting LUCY*) If you do that, I doubt whether you'll ever see Janet again. (*After a moment, facing LUCY*) It's as simple as that. |
| LUCY:  | (*Quietly*) Clive, I know you saw Pelford because I found the photograph in your overcoat. I also heard your conversation … |
| CLIVE: | What conversation? |
| LUCY:  | You telephoned someone. You said "Tell Pelford I'll take the reservation." (*Moving nearer to CLIVE*) What did you mean? |
| CLIVE: | (*Turning from LUCY*) I'm going away for a little while. Quite apart from this business, I think it's a good idea anyway. While I'm away you can think about the divorce. If you still want to go through with it … |
| LUCY:  | (*Taking hold of CLIVE's arm again*) Clive, don't lie! Don't evade the issue! (*Tensely*) What's this all about? |
| CLIVE: | (*Quietly*) Yesterday morning you said Janet was the only thing that mattered. I think so, too, Lucy. It's because I think that way that … |
| LUCY:  | (*Emotionally*) If you don't tell me the truth … if you don't tell me what happened last night, I shall go to Kenton … |
| CLIVE: | (*Releasing himself, interrupting her*) I've told you what will happen if you go to the police. (*He turns and picks up his suitcase and overcoat*) It's up to you, Lucy. |

*LUCY watches CLIVE as he walks towards the door.*

| LUCY:  | (*Quietly*) Where are you going? |
|--------|-----|

155

CLIVE:     I'm going abroad …
LUCY:      (*Desperately worried*) Where? For how long?
*CLIVE moves nearer the door. He hesitates and then turns*
*for a moment and looks at LUCY.*
CLIVE:     (*Quietly, look at LUCY*) Goodbye, Lucy.
LUCY:      Clive, wait a minute! (*After a moment*) Last
           night, while you were out, I started thinking
           about us. About Janet and … Well, you know
           how it is sometimes, you find yourself thinking
           of something, and then quite out of the blue,
           you remember something else … something
           quite different. I started thinking about Amalfi.
           The first time we went there, just before the
           war. Long before Janet was born. Do you
           remember?
CLIVE:     Yes, I remember …
LUCY:      That tiny bedroom, and the horrible wallpaper.
           It was facing the harbour and every morning a
           funny little man with blue jeans …
CLIVE:     (*Stopping LUCY*) Lucy, you didn't think of
           Amalfi four weeks ago, when we were talking
           about divorce …
LUCY:      (*Near to tears*) Neither of us thought of it …
CLIVE:     (*Softly*) I know … I know …
*LUCY starts to cry and turns away from CLIVE. He looks*
*at her and then goes out carrying his suitcase. There is a*
*pause. LUCY turns and looks towards the hall. Then she*
*moves to the settee. After a moment she moves back to the*
*small table and picks up a cigarette. She lifts the lighter,*
*but it refuses to work again, and she replaces both the*
*lighter and the cigarette on the table. Mixed with her*
*obvious emotion is a feeling of agitation. From outside*
*there is the sound of a car starting and being driven away.*
*LUCY crosses to the French windows and looks out into*

*the garden. As the sound of the car fades, she turns and moves to the telephone. She puts her hand on the instrument, hesitates, is desperately undecided whether to ring KENTON or not. Suddenly she picks up the receiver and starts to dial. We hear the number dialling out. The receiver is lifted at the other end.*

BAILEY:      Beacherscross Police Station …

LUCY:      Could I speak to Inspector Kenton, please?

BAILEY:      Who is that speaking?

LUCY:      (*Hesitating, then*) Mrs Freeman …

BAILEY:      One moment, please …

*LAURENCE HUDSON's voice can be heard from the background. He is standing in the entrance to the hall.*

LAURENCE:  Lucy … may I come in?

*LAURENCE is standing in the doorway with ANNA. He is carrying his hat and overcoat, together with a newspaper and valise.*

ANNA:      (*To LUCY*) Mr Hudson would like to see you, madam …

LUCY:      (*Surprised and relieved*) Oh, Laurence, you're just the person I want to see! (*To ANNA*) It's all right, Anna.

*ANNA goes out.*

KENTON:    (*On the other end of the line*) Good afternoon, Mrs Freeman. This is Inspector Kenton …

*LUCY looks at the receiver in her hand, then across at LAURENCE. Suddenly she replaces the telephone and moves towards LAURENCE. He is stood watching her, obviously bewildered.*

LAURENCE:  Lucy, what is it? What's the matter?

*LUCY covers her face with her hands. She is crying slightly. LAURENCE gently takes hold of her arm and moves her down to the settee. He waits a little while before speaking.*

LAURENCE:   (*Hesitant*) Has something happened, Lucy?

*LUCY nods.*

LAURENCE:   To Janet?

LUCY:   No … (*Looking up at him*) It's Clive … He saw Pelford last night … Laurence, I'm desperately worried …

LAURENCE:   (*Puzzled*) Why? What are you worried about? Lucy, tell me … what's happened?

LUCY:   Clive saw Pelford … They've agreed to release Janet … She's supposed to be coming home this afternoon …

LAURENCE:   (*Bewildered*) Well, then … why are you upset? I don't understand this. (*He stops and stares at LUCY*) Have they arrested Clive?

LUCY:   (*Surprised*) Arrested him? What for?

LAURENCE:   (*Indicating the newspaper he is carrying*) For the Nelson murder. There's a report here that …

LUCY:   No … No, it's not that.

LAURENCE:   Well, what is it, Lucy?

LUCY:   Clive's going away … He's going abroad somewhere …

LAURENCE:   Lucy, are you sure?

LUCY:   Yes. That's why Janet's coming home … Clive's come to some kind of an arrangement with Pelford. I don't know what it is but I'm sure …

*She is interrupted by the ringing of the telephone. LAURENCE looks towards the desk.*

LUCY:          That's probably the Inspector. I was just
               going to talk to him when you arrived …

*LAURENCE looks at LUCY then crosses to the desk and
picks up the receiver.*

LAURENCE:   (*On phone*) Beacherscross 189 …

KENTON:     (*On the other end*) Is that Mr Freeman?

LAURENCE:   No … this is Laurence Hudson …

KENTON:     (*Pleasantly*) Oh, good afternoon, Mr
            Hudson. This is Inspector Kenton. I
            believe Mrs Freeman was trying to get in
            touch with me and we were cut off …

*LAURENCE looks across at Lucy, hesitates, then*:

LAURENCE:   Inspector, will you be in your office in
            about an hour's time?

KENTON:     It's possible. Why?

LAURENCE:   I want to talk to you.

KENTON:     (*A shade significantly, but quite polite*)
            About the murder … the man we found in
            Henshaw wood?

LAURENCE:   (*Quietly*) Yes.

KENTON:     I shall be here. (*He puts the receiver
            down*)

*LAURENCE looks at Lucy, slowly replaces the telephone
and crosses to her. He sits down on the arm of the settee.*

LAURENCE:   Now tell me about Clive. Tell me what
            happened last night, Lucy.


CUT TO: DETECTIVE   INSPECTOR   KENTON's
Office at Beacherscross Police Station. About an hour
later.

*A bored Kenton is sitting behind his desk listening to Lady
Barbara Barstow who is sat facing him and is obviously
airing a considerable grievance.*

BARBARA: (*Annoyed*) … Well, if the police can't do anything about it … who can?

KENTON: I suggest you write to the local Council.

BARBARA: Do you think I haven't written to the Council? I wrote four letters last week!

KENTON: (*Rising*) I'm sorry Lady Barstow, it's private property and there's just nothing we can do.

BARBARA: (*Rising*) Well, I think it's positively disgraceful! Those wretched horses! How would you like it if they came pushing their way into your front garden?

KENTON: I shouldn't like it at all, Lady Barstow … but I can't quite see what I could do about it.

*SERGEANT CROSS enters.*

BARBARA: Well, I shall do something about it. I shall erect an enormous electric fence!

KENTON: (*To CROSS*) Yes, Sergeant?

CROSS: Mr Hudson, sir.

KENTON: (*Nodding*) Show him in.

*BARBARA moves towards the door.*

BARBARA: Some people seem to have no sense of responsibility whatsoever! It's beyond me! Quite beyond me!

KENTON: Have you spoken to Major Johnson?

BARBARA: Spoken to him! I might just as well talk to the horses!

*LAURENCE enters.*

KENTON: Come in, Mr Hudson.

LAURENCE: (*Surprised at seeing Barbara*) Oh, hello, Lady Barstow!

*BARBARA looks at him, gives a brief nod of recognition, murmurs "Good afternoon" and goes out.*

160

KENTON:        (*Smiling, indicating the chair*) Sit down, sir.

*LAURENCE sits facing the desk. KENTON returns to his chair and looks at LAURENCE.*

KENTON:        What is it you want to see me about?

LAURENCE:      (*A shade nervous*) I want to make a statement about the Nelson murder.

KENTON:        (*Politely*) The Nelson murder, Mr Hudson?

LAURENCE:      Yes. The man you found in Henshaw Wood.

KENTON:        (*After a moment*) Go on …

LAURENCE:      (*Obviously a shade nervous*) Nelson was an associate of Pelford's. He was concerned with the disappearance of Janet Freeman. He turned up at Amberley one night. You see, there was some suggestion that he and Clive might be able to …

KENTON:        (*Interrupting LAURENCE*) I can see the point of the visit, Mr Hudson. Just confine yourself to the facts. What happened?

LAURENCE:      (*Faintly surprised and puzzled by KENTON's manner: hesitant*) Well … Nelson discovered that I was there, in the Sun Lounge. He was annoyed because the house was supposed to be empty. He pulled a revolver out of his pocket … there was a struggle and … he was shot.

KENTON:        Accidentally?

LAURENCE:      Yes. Yes, of course.

KENTON:        Go on …

LAURENCE:      We were both terribly confused. We didn't know what on earth to do. Clive didn't want to go to the police because he thought if he did Pelford would get to know about it and … (*Not too sure of himself*) Well, for obvious reasons, he didn't want Pelford to think he'd double-crossed him.

*KENTON looks at LAURENCE, picks up a pencil and starts to doodle on his blotting pad.*

KENTON:      Go on …

LAURENCE:   (*Faintly embarrassed*) Well, I think you can guess what happened next.

KENTON:      I'd prefer you to tell me, Mr Hudson.

LAURENCE:   We took the body down to Henshaw Wood.

KENTON:      We? You mean … yourself and Mr Freeman?

LAURENCE:   Yes.

KENTON:      What time was that?

LAURENCE:   Oh, about half past ten. Perhaps a little later.

KENTON:      (*Quietly*) And the man was dead?

LAURENCE:   (*Surprised by the question*) Why yes, of course.

KENTON:      How do you know? Did you examine the body?

LAURENCE:   Why, yes.

KENTON:      When?

LAURENCE:   Before we left the house …

KENTON:      (*Quietly*) I see.

LAURENCE:   There was a button missing off his jacket … it came off during the struggle. You probably remember, you found it in the drawing room …

KENTON:      (*Non-committal*) Yes, I remember. Go on, Mr Hudson …

162

LAURENCE: Well, that's about all, so far as I'm concerned.

KENTON: You mean … that's all you want to tell me? There's nothing else?

LAURENCE: No, there is something else, Inspector. Something Mrs Freeman told me this afternoon. (*He rises, obviously a shade worried*) Whether it's true or not, I don't know.

KENTON: What did she tell you?

LAURENCE: She told me Clive saw Pelford again last night. She seems to think they've reached an agreement.

KENTON: About the child?

LAURENCE: Yes. Janet's supposed to be coming home this afternoon. According to Clive, she'll be on the four o'clock train …

KENTON: Did Mr Freeman tell <u>you</u> that?

LAURENCE: No, I haven't seen Clive. He told Lucy. Incidentally, she asked me not to tell you that. She's terrified in case something goes wrong …

KENTON: (*Nodding*) That's all right. Go on, Mr Hudson …

LAURENCE: Lucy's worried … She doesn't know what Clive's promised Pelford. She's sure it isn't just a question of money …

KENTON: Well, if it isn't money … what is it?

LAURENCE: I don't know, Inspector. All I know is Clive left for the Continent this afternoon and Lucy's worried … desperately worried.

*There is a slight pause. KENTON appears thoughtful yet strangely unimpressed.*

KENTON:       (*Looking up, simply*) Why?

LAURENCE:     (*Puzzled*) I beg your pardon?

KENTON:       I said … why? Why is Mrs Freeman worried?

LAURENCE:     (*A shade surprised by KENTON's apparent denseness*) Well, obviously she thinks this trip to the Continent's got something to do with Pelford and      the return of Janet. She's worried in case … well, in case something happens to Clive, or she never sees him again.

KENTON:       But I thought the Freemans were rather, well … How can I put this? … Rather at loggerheads.

LAURENCE:     They were. There was even talk of a divorce a few weeks ago, but the situation's changed rather          …

KENTON:       I'm delighted to hear it. (*He rises from his chair and moves round the desk*) Is there anything else, Mr Hudson?

LAURENCE:     (*Puzzled, even a little confused by KENTON's manner*) No, no I don't think so.

KENTON:       (*Quite pleasantly*) There's nothing you've forgotten?

LAURENCE:     No …

KENTON:       Well, I'm most grateful to you for coming along. (*Smiles and shakes hands*) You've been very frank, and I appreciate it, sir.

*SERGEANT CROSS enters with a folder which he places on the desk.*

KENTON:       (*To CROSS*) Mr Hudson's leaving, Sergeant.

CROSS: Very good, sir. (*He crosses and opens the door for LAURENCE*)

LAURENCE: (*Still a shade bewildered by KENTON's manner*) Goodbye, Inspector.

KENTON: (*Apparently interested in the folder, not looking at LAURENCE*) Good afternoon, sir.

*LAURENCE goes out with SERGEANT CROSS. As the door closes KENTON looks up, losing all interest in the folder on his desk. He sits in his chair, picks up his pipe and puts it in his mouth. After a moment he takes the pipe out of his mouth again and starts tapping his teeth with it. He looks thoughtful, and a shade disturbed.*

CUT TO: The entrance to London airport. Afternoon.

*CLIVE arrives in a private-hire car, gets out of the car, pays the driver then takes a suitcase off the back seat and crosses into the main departure building. He looks a shade tired and distinctly worried. PELFORD is sitting in a small car, watching CLIVE enter the departure building. PELFORD gets out of his car, obviously rather pleased with himself. He crosses the road towards a telephone box. He goes into it and inserts coins and dials a number. As he waits for the number to ring out, he glances through the window at the airport building. We hear the number ringing out at the other end, and after a little while the receiver is lifted.*

CUT TO: A small bed-sitting room.

This is an untidy room with a bed, settee, several chairs and a built-in wardrobe. There is a window facing the square. A telephone is on the dressing table facing the door.

*LOMAX is standing by a table. He is holding the telephone. He still wears glasses and a bow tie.*

LOMAX:     Hello? Freemantle 0734 …

PELFORD:   (*On the other end after pressing button A*) Is that you, Lomax?

LOMAX:     Yes …

PELFORD:   This is Pelford …

LOMAX:     (*Anxiously*) What's happened?

PELFORD:   It's ok. He's arrived. Tell Lynn to put the child on the train.

LOMAX:     Right!


CUT TO: *PELFORD leaving the telephone box and crossing towards the airport building. He still looks pleased with himself, then suddenly, as he reaches the pavement in front of the main entrance, a car races in front of him and brakes to a standstill. It is a police car. Two plainclothes men jump out of the car, take hold of PELFORD and before he realises what is happening, he is sitting in the back of the car next to a uniformed POLICE INSPECTOR. The car makes a speedy departure.*


CUT TO: A Victorian house in a quiet square off the Cromwell Road, London. Stone steps lead up to the front door of the house.

*A Mercedes Benz car drives up to the house and as it does so the front door opens, and we see LYNN, LOMAX and JANET FREEMAN standing in the doorway. There is a bandage over JANET's eyes.*

LOMAX:     (*To LYNN*) It's the 3.10 from Marylebone. Put her on the train and get back here as soon as you can.

166

*LYNN nods, takes hold of JANET's arm and quickly takes her down the steps towards the waiting car. LOMAX closes the door.*

CUT TO: The bed sitting room.
*LOMAX enters, locks the door behind him and crosses to the built-in cupboard, lifts a concealed shutter and we see that the cupboard contains a shortwave radio transmitter. He switches on the set and then crosses to the dressing-table and takes a notebook out of one of the drawers. He slowly returns to the cupboard, studying the notebook. After a moment he consults his wristwatch, then draws up a chair and places it in front of the radio set. At that moment, the telephone rings. He turns, hesitates, then crosses to the dressing-table and picks up the telephone.*

| | |
|---|---|
| LOMAX: | (*On phone*) Hello? Freemantle 0734 … |
| STEVENS: | (*On the other end; tensely*) Lomax? |
| LOMAX: | (*Surprised*) Yes … |
| STEVENS: | This is Stevens … Lomax, listen! They've picked up Pelford – there's a complete change of plan … |
| LOMAX: | (*Interrupting him, stunned*) What do you mean – picked him up? |
| STEVENS: | The police picked him up at the Airport about half-an-hour ago. Now, Lomax, listen – don't do anything about the Freeman child. I'll phone you tonight as soon as … |
| LOMAX: | What d'you mean – don't do anything! She's gone! She left five minutes ago! |

CUT TO: The main hall at Marylebone Station.
*LYNN and JANET FREEMAN cross the hall towards the ticket collector and the entrance to a departure platform.*

*The bandage has been removed from JANET's eyes. LYNN presents her tickets, and they pass through the barrier onto the platform. There is a waiting train for Beacherscross. LYNN walks down the platform with JANET. Eventually she discovers an empty 1st class compartment. She opens the carriage door and JANET climbs into the train. The Station Clock shows that it is nearly ten minutes past three.*

CUT TO: The entrance to Marylebone Station.
*A taxi drives up to the station and before it comes to a standstill LOMAX jumps out of the cab, throws a ten-shilling note at the driver and rushes into the station.*

CUT TO: The Platform.
*The train is on the verge of departure. Doors are being slammed. The GUARD's whistle can be heard. The train slowly begins to move. LYNN has turned her back on the train and is walking quickly towards the barrier. LOMAX appears at the barrier. The TICKET COLLECTOR tries to restrain him from entering the platform, but he pushes the COLLECTOR to one side and races past an astonished LYNN towards the quickly departing train. LOMAX races down the platform in a desperate attempt to catch the last coach.*

CUT TO: A platform at Beacherscross Station.
*LUCY and LAURENCE are on the platform, awaiting the arrival of the train. The train can be seen in the distance, approaching the station. The train arrives, and as the passengers alight, LUCY runs up and down the train in a desperate attempt to find JANET. LAURENCE climbs into the train and quickly rushes down the corridor, searching the various carriages. LUCY runs along the platform in*

*search of JANET. Eventually LAURENCE gets out of the train and joins LUCY on the platform. He looks tense and worried. He takes LUCY by the arm and slowly shakes his head. The train begins to move away from the platform.*

CUT TO: *A London taxi draws to a standstill in front of the entrance to a London Underground station. LOMAX gets out of the taxi with JANET. He is holding her hand and she has obviously been crying.*

DRIVER: (*Feeling in his pockets for change, casually*) What's the matter with the kiddie?

LOMAX: She's had toothache all morning. I'm taking her to the dentist.

*The DRIVER nods and gives LOMAX his change. LOMAX and JANET go down into the entrance of the Tube station.*

CUT TO: *The Mercedes car draws to a standstill outside of the Victorian house in the Square off the Cromwell Road.*
*LOMAX gets out of the car towards the steps leading up to the house. As they reach the top step the door is opened by LYNN. LOMAX and JANET disappear into the house. The Mercedes car makes a quick getaway. We then focus on the house opposite on the other side of the Square. The top bedroom window is covered by lace curtains, but we see the figure of a man cautiously looking down at the house opposite.*

CUT TO: The interior of this room. It is a large bedroom that has obviously been converted into a vantage point from which to watch the house opposite. A table stands at right-angles to the window and on this table is an open tape recorder, two telephones, a short-wave radio receiving set and a tray containing cups of tea and the remains of a meal.

*A plainclothes police sergeant – SERGEANT DAVIS – sits at this table, holding the telephone receiver to his ear. SUPERINTENDENT WILDE stands by the window, binoculars in hand, staring at the house on the other side of the Square.*

CROSS:     (*On the other end of the phone*) Beacherscross Police Station …

DAVIS:     Put me through to Inspector Kenton, please …

*He turns and hands the receiver to SUPERINTENDENT WILDE who takes it, but still stands looking out of the window at the house opposite. After a moment we hear KENTON's voice on the other end of the line.*

KENTON: Inspector Kenton speaking …

WILDE:     (*Turning from the window; on the phone*) Hello, Kenton – this is Wilde.

KENTON: Any news, sir?

WILDE:     (*Quietly*) Yes. They've just brought her back to the house …

# END OF EPISODE FIVE

# EPISODE SIX

OPEN TO: The Bedroom.

*DETECTIVE SUPERINTENDENT WILDE is on the telephone talking to KENTON. SERGEANT DAVIS is watching and listening to the conversation.*

KENTON: (*On the other end*) Inspector Kenton speaking.

WILDE: (*Turning from the window; on the phone*) Hello, Kenton – this is Wilde.

KENTON: Any news, sir?

WILDE: (*Quietly*) Yes. They've just brought her back to the house …

KENTON: (*Obviously relieved*) Oh, thank heaven for that!

WILDE: What about Pelford?

KENTON: I'm afraid we can't get anything out of him, sir.

WILDE: (*Quite calmly*) Yes, well, don't worry, Kenton … he'll talk eventually.

KENTON: I'm not worried about Pelford. I'm worried about        the child. If anything goes wrong …

WILDE: (*Stopping him; a note of authority*) Nothing's going to go wrong. (*Quite friendly*) How did you get on this afternoon?

KENTON: I told him the whole story. He only left about half an hour ago.

WILDE: How did he take it?

KENTON: Very well, I think, but he's terribly worried. So am I, if it comes to that.

WILDE: Yes, I know.

KENTON: We're taking a hell of a risk, sir.

WILDE: You know the next move, Kenton?

KENTON: Yes.

WILDE: All right. Keep in touch … let me know what happens.

KENTON: Yes, sir.

*WILDE replaces the receiver, looks out of the window, then turns towards SERGEANT DAVIS. He looks at his*

173

*wristlet watch, then at DAVIS again. He is serious, thoughtful.*

WILDE:      (*After a moment*) If nothing happens by ten o'clock, we'll move in …

DAVIS:      (*Nodding*) Yes, sir.

*DAVIS turns and picks up the second telephone receiver on the desk. WILDE raises his binoculars and looks out of the window.*

CUT TO:   The Drawing Room at Amberley.

*LAURENCE HUDSON is at the drinks table, mixing a brandy and soda. He eventually takes the drink to LUCY who is sitting on the settee. She looks tired and drawn.*

LUCY:       (*Taking the drink, distressed*) … It's perfectly obvious they hadn't the slightest intention of putting Janet on the train. They lied to Clive! They must have lied to him otherwise …

LAURENCE:  (*Interrupting her*) I don't know, Lucy. I just can't make it out …

LUCY:       (*Looking up at LAURENCE, surprised and a shade tense*) What do you mean, Laurence?

*LAURENCE hesitates but doesn't reply.*

LUCY:       Do you mean Clive wasn't telling the truth?

LAURENCE:  (*Turning away from the settee, faintly irritated*) I don't know whether he was telling the truth or not. The fact remains she wasn't on the train …

*LUCY looks at LAURENCE, obviously a shade surprised.*

LUCY:       Laurence, you don't think Clive had anything to do with Janet disappearing? You don't think he was a friend of

**174**

Pelford's and knew all the time that Janet
...

LAURENCE: (*Turning towards the settee again, interrupting LUCY*) No. No, of course not, Lucy! You mustn't even think things like that.

LUCY: What did Kenton say this afternoon? ... About Clive, I mean?

LAURENCE: He didn't say anything about Clive. The Inspector's a curious man, I can't quite weigh him up. I told him what happened the night Nelson came here and he ... (*He suddenly stops speaking and turns towards the door*)

*LUCY realises LA|URENCE is looking at someone and quickly turns. CLIVE is standing in the doorway, suitcase in hand. He is wearing his hat, his overcoat is thrown over his right shoulder.*

CLIVE: (*Quietly*) Hello, Lucy ... Laurence ...

LUCY: Clive!

*CLIVE comes into the room, takes off his hat and coat and puts down the suitcase. LUCY moves towards him.*

LUCY: Clive, what happened?

CLIVE: (*Sitting on the arm of the settee, obviously weary*) No one turned up at the airport ... I waited until four o'clock ... (*Looks up at LUCY*) I suppose Janet wasn't on the train?

LUCY: (*Shaking her head*) No ...

CLIVE: And no one's telephoned?

*LUCY shakes her head again.*

LAURENCE: (*Moving towards CLIVE*) Clive, have you seen Kenton?

175

| CLIVE: | (*Surprised by the question*) No, I've come straight from the airport. Why should I see Kenton? |
|---|---|
| LAURENCE: | I thought perhaps he … He knows about Nelson … he knows exactly what happened that night. |
| CLIVE: | How does he know? |
| LAURENCE: | I told him the whole story. |
| CLIVE: | When? |
| LAURENCE: | This afternoon … |
| CLIVE: | (*Looking at LAURENCE, obviously curious*) What time did you see Kenton? |
| LAURENCE: | (*Faintly puzzled*) About two … perhaps a little later. Why? |

*CLIVE suddenly rises from the settee. He is agitated.*

| LUCY: | Clive, what is it … what's the matter? |
|---|---|
| CLIVE: | (*On edge, tensely*) Pelford intended to play fair over this, I'm sure he did. He gave me his word that Janet would be on the four o'clock train. (*To LAURENCE angrily*) You shouldn't have gone to the police until Janet was safe – here, in the house! |

*LAURENCE looks at CLIVE, obviously perplexed.*

| LUCY: | You think they found out about Laurence? You think that's why Janet wasn't on the train? |
|---|---|
| CLIVE: | Yes, I do. They probably thought I was double crossing them and had … |

*CLIVE is interrupted by the ringing of the telephone. LUCY, LAURENCE and CLIVE instinctively turn towards the desk. CLIVE moves to the desk and lifts the receiver. He puts the receiver to his ear, looking across at LUCY and LAURENCE. From the other end of the line we hear the sound of button A being pressed and the dropping of*

176

*coins. During the following conversation LAURENCE and LUCY move towards CLIVE.*

CLIVE:      Hello?

STEVENS:    (*On the other end, curtly*) Is that you, Freeman?

CLIVE:      (*Puzzled*) Yes … Who is this?

STEVENS:    (*A note of sarcasm in his voice, controlling his annoyance*) This is Stevens … Robert Stevens …

CLIVE:      (*Tensely*) Look, Stevens … what happened this afternoon? Janet wasn't on the train and Pelford didn't …

STEVENS:    (*Interrupting him*) What happened this afternoon? You know what happened! They picked Pelford up  …

CLIVE:      (*Bewildered*) Who picked him up?

STEVENS:    (*Angrily*) The Police! You let us down, Freeman. You told that slick lawyer friend of yours to see Kenton while you deliberately …

CLIVE:      (*Interrupting him, tensely*) Stevens, I didn't! I swear to you I didn't!

STEVENS:    Well, what happened?

CLIVE:      (*Anxiously, desperately worried*) I don't know … I went to the airport and waited until four o'clock            …

STEVENS:    I don't believe you …

CLIVE:      Stevens, listen – Hudson went to the police without my knowing about it … that's the truth – I swear to you it's the truth.

*There is a slight pause: STEVENS does not reply.*

CLIVE:      Are you there? Stevens?

STEVENS:          (*After a moment, quietly*) Freeman, if we
                  return the child – tonight – are you still
                  prepared to go through with this? Are you
                  still prepared to go to Hamburg?
CLIVE:            (*Tensely*) Yes, of course, I've already told
                  you that!
STEVENS:          I'll ring you back in half an hour.
*STEVENS replaces the receiver at his end. CLIVE puts the
telephone down and turns away from the desk.*
LAURENCE:  (*To CLIVE*) What's happening?
CLIVE:            He's    ringing    back   …   (*Looking   at
                  LAURENCE*) The police picked up Pelford
                  – that's why Janet wasn't on the train …
LAURENCE:  When did this happen?
CLIVE:            This  afternoon  …  They  thought  I  was
                  responsible, they thought it was through
                  me you went to the police.
LUCY:             But how did they know about Laurence?
CLIVE:            I  don't  know.  (*To  LAURENCE*)  Who
                  knew you were going to see the Inspector
                  this afternoon?
LAURENCE:  No one, except Lucy …
CLIVE:            (*To LUCY*) Did you tell anyone?
LUCY:             No, of course I didn't …
CLIVE:            (*To LAURENCE*) Did you see anyone – at
                  the station, I mean?
LAURENCE:  (*Thoughtfully*) Why, no … only the local
                  Sergeant, and Kenton, of course. (*Puzzled*)
                  I don't understand this. I'm sure my going
                  to see Kenton had   nothing  to  do  with
                  Pelford's arrest …
CLIVE:            But didn't you tell Kenton I'd gone to the
                  airport?

178

LAURENCE: No, I didn't. I simply said you'd left for the Continent. As a matter of fact, I gave him the impression you'd already gone.

LUCY: Clive, do you think this is going to make a difference to Janet? Do you think they'll now decide to ...

CLIVE: (*Interrupting her*) I think they've every intention of returning Janet, providing I do what they want me to do. So far as they're concerned, Janet's simply a means to an end. (*Looks at LAURENCE*) But, if there's a repetition of what happened this afternoon, I wouldn't like to say ...

LAURENCE: (*Annoyed, interrupting him*) Look, Clive, you can't blame me for what happened this afternoon. Lucy was telephoning Kenton when I arrived here.

CLIVE: (*To LUCY*) Is this true?

LUCY: (*After a moment*) Yes.

CLIVE: But I warned you not to contact Kenton. I told you it was a risk – a big risk!

LUCY: (*Looking at CLIVE*) It was a risk I was prepared to take.

CLIVE: (*Moving nearer to LUCY*) Look, Lucy, we've got to face it. The police won't get Janet back for us ... they've tried and they've failed.

LAURENCE: I wouldn't under-rate the police if I were you, Clive. After all they've picked up Pelford.

CLIVE: And where does that get them?

LAURENCE: Well, if Pelford talks ...

CLIVE: (*Impatiently*) Pelford won't talk, I'm sure of that.

179

LAURENCE: What makes you so sure?

CLIVE: The fact that Stevens rang me this afternoon. If they'd been worried about Pelford they wouldn't have contacted me. They'd have had other things to think about.

LAURENCE: (*Thoughtfully*) I don't know. I'm not so sure about that.

CLIVE: Laurence, what exactly did you tell Kenton?

LAURENCE: I told him what happened the night Nelson came here.

CLIVE: Was he surprised?

LAURENCE: (*A shade puzzled*) No, curiously enough, I don't think he was. He gave me the impression that he already knew about Nelson.

*ANNA enters from the hall.*

LUCY: (*To ANNA*) Yes, Anna?

ANNA: There's a gentleman to see Mr Freeman, ma'am. He says it's important.

CLIVE: Well, who is it?

ANNA: (*To CLIVE*) He says his name's Trafford and he's got a message for you, sir. He won't give me the message. I've asked him.

CLIVE: Trafford?

ANNA: I think it was Trafford, or Stafford ... I'm not sure.

CLIVE: (*Recognising the name*) Stafford? All right, Anna ... ask him in.

*ANNA goes out.*

LUCY: (*To CLIVE*)   Who is it?

CLIVE: Well, I don't know. There used to be a chap at Prescott called Stafford. He was one of the Special Messengers.

*CLIVE, LUCY and LAURENCE turn towards the door as JACK STAFFORD enters. He is a Government Despatch Rider. He wears the uniform of a despatch rider and carries his crash helmet. Attached to his belt is a wallet-pouch. He takes an envelope out of the pouch as he enters the room.*

CLIVE: (*Pleasantly, recognising him*) Hello, Stafford! I wondered if it was you.

STAFFORD: Nice to see you again, Mr Freeman. I hope you've been keeping well, sir … (*Hesitant*) In spite of everything.

CLIVE: Yes, thank you, Stafford.

*STAFFORD nods to LUCY and LAURENCE and hands CLIVE the envelope.*

STAFFORD: Mr Miller asked me to deliver this, sir. He said it was important. I understand he's phoning you tomorrow morning.

CLIVE: Oh, I see. (*He looks at the envelope and then at STAFFORD*) Have you just come from Prescott?

STAFFORD: Yes, sir. I left just after two o'clock.

LAURENCE: Two o'clock? That's pretty good going …

STAFFORD: Yes, sir. I didn't stop for tea …

CLIVE: (*With a little smile*) Yes, well I expect we can manage of cup of tea, Stafford. (*To LUCY*) Lucy, do you think Anna could …

LUCY: Yes, of course! (*To STAFFORD*) Come along, Mr Stafford.

*STAFFORD smiles, nods to LAURENCE and CLIVE and goes out with LUCY. CLIVE stands looking at the envelope. After a moment's hesitation he rips it open and*

181

*takes out a letter and two sheets of typed notepaper. He quickly reads the letter and then glances at the accompanying notes. He puts the letter back into the envelope and then crosses towards the picture on the far wall.*

LAURENCE: (*Smiling*) Is it as important as the gentleman from Mars seems to imagine?

*CLIVE swings the picture away from the wall and takes out his keys.*

CLIVE: (*His thoughts obviously elsewhere*) Hm? What did you say?

LAURENCE: I said is it important?

CLIVE: (*Thoughtfully; unlocking the safe*) It's always important when a man like Miller changes his mind. (*He takes the envelope out of his pocket and puts it into the safe*)

LAURENCE: Is Miller the head of Prescott?

CLIVE: Well, ostensibly. He's in charge of the research departments. (*Closing the safe and locking it*) Three years ago Miller and I had a disagreement. We were both working on a moulding process, rather on the lines of the Riverdale Press ...

LAURENCE: Yes, I remember. You told Inspector Kenton.

CLIVE: (*Turning*) Did I? When?

LAURENCE: The night Nelson came. Don't you remember? He questioned you about Prescott, and that chap who disappeared ... Bramwell something-or-other.

CLIVE: Bramwell-Cane. Yes, of course. I remember now.

LAURENCE: Wasn't Cane a traitor? Didn't he leave Prescott because ...

CLIVE:          (*Interrupting him, a shade tense*) Cane
                was a scientist – a first class scientist. He
                wasn't appreciated at Prescott so went
                elsewhere. You can't call a man a traitor
                just because …

LAURENCE:   (*Quietly, watching CLIVE*) Is that what
                Pelford and Co want you to do, Clive …
                go elsewhere?

CLIVE:          Yes. They want me to go to Hamburg and
                then presumably on to Prague. At least
                that's what they say. But my bet is these
                people have no political affiliations, no
                contact with Bramwell-Cane or anything
                else in authority. They simply intend to
                sell me to the highest bidder.

LAURENCE:   But how can they do that if you refuse?

CLIVE:          How can I refuse, Laurence? If I stay in
                England, ten to one I'll find myself facing
                a murder charge. Besides, lets face the
                facts. If I don't do what they want me to
                do, neither Lucy nor I will ever see Janet
                again. Even now there's a doubt in my
                mind. A terrible doubt …

LAURENCE:   A doubt?

CLIVE:          (*Hesitant*) I wouldn't say this to Lucy, so
                for God's sake don't repeat it, but … I
                doubt whether Janet's still alive.

LAURENCE:   Why do you say that?

CLIVE:          I don't know. I didn't like the way Stevens
                sounded to me on the telephone. It seemed
                to me that … (*Desperately worried*)
                Perhaps I'm wrong. Perhaps it's just my
                imagination.

LAURENCE: I'm sure it is. (*He looks at CLIVE*) You know, I often think it's a pity you ever left Prescott, Clive. Things haven't really worked out, have they?

CLIVE: (*Still a shade angry and irritated*) I refuse to look at the past through a nostalgic haze. I wasn't happy at Prescott. Miller was always on my tail. I couldn't do a damn thing without his interfering. (*With a nod towards the picture on the wall*) Anyway, he's had the decency to admit he was wrong … that's something, I suppose.

LAURENCE: Do they want you to go back?

CLIVE: Yes. Just between you and me, Laurence, they've offered me a Department – with no interference from Mr Miller, guaranteed.

LAURENCE: Has Miller written to you to that effect?

CLIVE: Yes.

LAURENCE: My word, they must need you badly.

CLIVE: (*Nodding*) They're trying a new process based on my Riverdale experiments. Miller's sent me the details. It's just up my street.

*LUCY enters from the hall. LAURENCE turns, takes out his watch and glances at it.*

LAURENCE: I'm going back to Town, Clive. If Stevens telephones and you want me to do anything, let me know.

CLIVE: Yes, all right.

LUCY: I'll see you out, Laurence.

*LUCY goes out into the hall with LAURENCE. CLIVE moves to the table, takes a cigarette from the box, then changes his mind and replaces it. He crosses and sits*

184

*down on the settee. He looks worried and thoughtful. After a moment LUCY returns.*

LUCY:     Clive, you shouldn't have lost your temper with Laurence. He's been awfully decent about things, you know.

CLIVE:    (*Still obviously a shade tense, not looking at LUCY*) Yes, I'm sorry, Lucy.

*LUCY looks at CLIVE, hesitates, and then moves towards him. CLIVE turns and faces her. There is a pause. CLIVE is obviously thinking of something. After a moment and to LUCY's surprise he takes hold of her arm.*

LUCY:     (*Hesitant*) Clive, do you think everything's going to be all right – with Janet?

*CLIVE looks at LUCY, hesitates and gives a little nod.*

LUCY:     No, Clive, please … what do you really think?

CLIVE:    (*Quietly*) Try not to worry, Lucy.

*CLIVE lifts LUCY's hand and kisses it. LUCY looks at him, puzzled and obviously worried.*


CUT TO:   WILDE's Headquarters.

*SERGEANT DAVIS is sitting at the table. There is a buzz-buzz from the telephone receiver and DAVIS picks it up. SUPERINTENDENT WILDE turns from the window and looks across at DAVIS.*

DAVIS:    (*On phone*) Hello?

OPERATOR: (*Briskly, on the other end of the line*) He's on the line again. He's ringing the Beacherscross number …

DAVIS:    Put him through … (*He turns and speaks to WILDE as he switches on the tape recorder*) He's phoning Freeman again, sir.

WILDE:    (*Nodding and moving to the table*) Right!

185

CUT TO:   The Drawing Room at Amberley.

*The telephone on the desk is ringing. CLIVE picks up the receiver. LUCY is anxiously watching him from the settee.*

CLIVE:      (*On phone*) Beacherscross 189 …

STEVENS:   (*On the other end*) Freeman?

CLIVE:      Yes …

STEVENS:   This is Stevens …

CLIVE:      Well?

STEVENS:   Freeman … we've reached a decision. We don't think you had anything to do with this afternoon …

CLIVE:      I've already told you that.

STEVENS:   So, if you're prepared to do what we want …

CLIVE:      (*Interrupting him, tensely, yet with a note of weariness*) Stevens, I'll do what the hell you want me to do …

STEVENS:   (*Pleased*) Good …

CLIVE:      … on one condition …

STEVENS:   (*Faintly surprised*) What's that?

CLIVE:      I've got to see my daughter – tonight.

STEVENS:   (*After a moment*) It's now a quarter past five … meet me at Cambridge Circus at six o'clock.

CLIVE:      Very well …

STEVENS:   Alone, Mr Freeman …

*CLIVE slowly replaces the receiver and looks across at LUCY who is anxiously watching him.*

CUT TO:   *CLIVE gets out of a taxi at Cambridge Circus, pays the driver, and strolls towards the Palace Theatre. He stands on the kerb, looking towards Charing Cross road.   After a moment he turns and strolls towards Shaftesbury Avenue. As he does so a Mercedes car appears and quickly draws to a standstill opposite where CLIVE is standing. The car door is thrown open and after a momentary hesitation CLIVE enters the car. The Mercedes drives round the island and heads off until it disappears down Charing Cross Road in the direction of Trafalgar Square. A van bearing the name J.W. JOHNSON & CO., Dry Cleaners, Clapham, follows closely behind the Mercedes.*

CUT TO: WILDE's Headquarters off the Cromwell Road.

*SUPERINTENDENT WILDE is standing by SERGEANT DAVIS who is still sitting by the table. DAVIS is wearing telephone style headphones and microphone and is listening to a man's voice over the shortwave radio. We can hear the voice, but it is impossible to tell what the man is saying. WILDE watches DAVIS as he quickly makes notes on a scribbling pad.*

DAVIS: (*To WILDE, looking up*) They picked him up in Cambridge Circus …

WILDE: Where are they now?

DAVIS: They're just off the Fulham Road, sir …

WILDE: Tell Sanders whatever happens they mustn't lose sight of him …

*DAVIS turns, flicks down a switch on the radio receiver and speaks into the microphone.*

DAVIS: Don't lose sight of him, Sanders … It's important … Over.

*DAVIS replaces the switch and we hear the man's voice again.*

DAVIS: (*To WILDE, after a moment*) They're heading for the Cromwell Road, sir …

WILDE: (*Nodding*) They're bringing him back to the house …

187

DAVIS: Yes, it looks like it, sir.

*WILDE turns and picks up one of the telephone receivers. He dials a number. We hear the number ringing out and then a man's voice on the other end of the line.*

BAILEY: Bailey, speaking …

WILDE: This is Wilde.

BAILEY: Yes, sir?

WILDE: Bailey, listen – they're bringing him back to the house. I think this is it.

BAILEY: Right, we're ready, sir.

WILDE: Make it seven o'clock. (*Looks at his wristlet watch*) I make it six thirty-four. Check?

BAILEY: Check …

*WILDE replaces the receiver and turns towards DAVIS. DAVIS is still listening to the man's voice.*

DAVIS: (*To WILDE*) They're just turning into Ennismore Gardens.

WILDE: Tell Sanders I've contacted Bailey. It's seven o'clock.

DAVIS: Yes, sir.

*WILDE picks up the second telephone and starts to dial.*

CUT TO: *The Mercedes car draws to a standstill in front of the house in the Square off the Cromwell Road. STEVENS gets out of the car, followed by CLIVE. The car drives away. CLIVE looks up at the house and then follows STEVENS up the stone steps to the front door.*

CUT TO: The Bed Sitting Room.
*LOMAX has just finished working the radio transmitter and is closing the shutters which conceal the instrument. He locks the cupboard doors and then turns back into the room. At this moment CLIVE enters followed by STEVENS.*

LOMAX: (*To STEVENS, a shade irritated*) You're just in time. There's been a message through from Hamburg.

STEVENS: Well?

LOMAX: The boat leaves Harwich at midnight. Our friend's meeting us at Ipswich.

STEVENS: (*Quietly*) Good. (*To LOMAX*) I think you'd better fetch the child.

LOMAX: (*Looking at CLIVE*) Wait a minute. (*To CLIVE*) Mr Freeman, your solicitor went to see Inspector Kenton this afternoon. Shortly afterwards a colleague of ours was arrested at London Airport.

CLIVE: (*Tensely, irritated*) That was none of my doing. I've already told Stevens that. Damn it, man, I went to the airport – I waited for Pelford!

LOMAX: (*Quietly, watching him*) I hope you're telling me the truth, Mr Freeman.

CLIVE: (*On edge, to STEVENS*) Who is this man?

LOMAX: My name is Lomax.

CLIVE: (*Turning towards LOMAX again, obviously irritated by him*) Well, listen, Mr Lomax, so far as I'm concerned this is a deal – and it takes two people to make a deal.

LOMAX: What do you mean?

CLIVE: You want me to go to Hamburg. Well, I'm not going to Hamburg or Harwich or anywhere else until I've seen my daughter.

*LOMAX looks at CLIVE. It is obvious he has taken an intense dislike to him. He sits on the arm of a chair.*

LOMAX: Mr Freeman, I think you're labouring under a delusion.

189

CLIVE:      (*Hesitant*) About … Janet?

LOMAX:      (*Shaking his head*) No, about yourself. (*He casually takes a small revolver out of his jacket pocket*) You're not in a position to issue instructions … to me, or to anyone else. You're at the receiving end of this deal, Mr Freeman. (*Casually, pointing the revolver at CLIVE*) You'll do precisely what we want you to do …

CLIVE:      (*Quite calmly, looking at LOMAX*) We'll discuss that when I've seen my daughter. (*He points to the revolver*) And I should put that away if I were you, just in case it goes off. (*With the suggestion of a smile*) I'm sure your friends would like me to remain in reasonably good health, Mr Lomax.

*LOMAX looks angry. He moves towards CLIVE, but STEVENS stops him.*

STEVENS:    Fetch the child …

*LOMAX hesitates, then turns away from CLIVE and goes out of the room. STEVENS takes out his cigarette case and helps himself to a cigarette.*

STEVENS:    I'm sorry about that. It won't happen again. He's a large fish in a small pool at the moment. The situation will change.

CLIVE:      (*Quietly*) I think so, too.

*STEVENS looks at CLIVE as he lights his cigarette, faintly surprised by his remark, then he turns towards the door. JANET is standing in the doorway with LYNN and LOMAX close behind her.*

JANET: Daddy! (*She rushes across the room towards her father. CLIVE takes her in his arms*)

190

CUT TO: *The van bearing the name J.W. Johnson & Co., Dry Cleaners, Clapham, draws to a standstill at the entrance to the Square off the Cromwell Road. The back doors of the van are thrown open and two uniformed policemen quickly emerge onto the road. They lift a "Diversion" road sign out of the parked van and place it in the middle of the road, thus closing the Square to oncoming traffic. A policeman remains with the sign and the second man climbs back into the van. The van continues down the Square.*

CUT TO: *A Police Car drives down a narrow lane at the rear of the house in the Square. The car stops and several uniformed and plainclothes police emerge from the car and take up positions facing the house. They are eliminating any possible means of escape from the back entrance. Two of the plainclothes men start to climb over the brick wall which surrounds the property.*

CUT TO: *The Dry Cleaning Van and two Police Cars arrive at the front entrance to the house in the Square. Uniformed and plainclothes men emerge from the cars and take up strategic positions. SUPERINTENDENT WILDE enters the Square from the house opposite. They join the group of Flying Squad men on the pavement. WILDE issues instructions and then together with two plainclothes officers he goes up the steps towards the house. At the front door WILDE rings the doorbell and waits for it to be answered. Suddenly the door is thrown open by LOMAX. He stares at the police in astonishment, and then suddenly turns and tries to disappear back into the house. The Flying Squad men spring forward and before LOMAX realises what is happening he is being forced down the steps towards the police car. WILDE and the other uniformed and plainclothes men enter the house. A man stands guard at the front door.*

CUT TO: The Drawing Room at Amberley. Later the same evening. The curtains are drawn across the French windows and the room is deserted.

*BARBARA BARSTOW enters from the hall followed by ANNA.*

ANNA:  (*A shade annoyed*) I'm not sure whether Mrs    Freeman is in or not.

BARBARA:  Well, perhaps you'll be good enough to find out.

*ANNA looks at BARBARA and hesitates.*

BARBARA:  Go on, I shan't steal anything …

ANNA:  (*Still hesitating*) Mrs Freeman hasn't been very well …

BARBARA:  (*Controlling her irritation*) I'm fully aware of that, Anna. Now just see if your mistress can spare me a few moments.

*ANNA hesitates, then goes out. BARBARA looks irritated, then gives a little shrug of indifference, and moves to the drinks table. She casually picks up a bottle, looks at the label and replaces it on the table. She moves about the room, inquisitively examining various objects. She picks up what looks like a letter but is disappointed to find that it is a receipt. She replaces the receipt and continues her tour of the room. Eventually she reaches the picture on the far wall. She stands looking at the picture for a moment, then reaches out as if to straighten it – or possibly swing it away from the wall? At that moment there is a noise from the French windows, and BARBARA swings round in surprise and faces the curtains. They are drawn aside and DETECTIVE INSPECTOR KENTON enters, having unlocked the French windows with a key from outside. He*

*is obviously surprised to see BARBARA. He draws the*
*curtains together and moves into the room.*

KENTON:  Good evening, Lady Barstow.

BARBARA:  What are you doing here?

KENTON:  I came to see Mrs Freeman.

BARBARA:  Do you usually come in through the French windows?

KENTON:  (*Pleasantly*) Occasionally. It breaks the monotony. Have you an appointment with Mrs Freeman?

BARBARA:  (*Surprised by the question*) No ... I just dropped in to have a chat.

KENTON:  Well, I'm afraid I must ask you to postpone your chat until tomorrow morning.

BARBARA:  Oh.

KENTON:  (*Looking at his watch*) I have an appointment with Mrs Freeman – it's rather important. I'm sure you understand, Lady Barstow.

BARBARA:  (*Puzzled*) Yes, yes, of course. (*A little laugh*) I only wanted to borrow a bottle of sherry, anyway.

KENTON:  Oh, I see. (*He looks at the drinks table, crosses, picks up a bottle and hands it to BARBARA*) I'll explain to Mrs Freeman. (*With charm*) It'll be quite all right, Lady Barstow, I'm sure.

BARBARA:  (*A little taken aback but taking the bottle from KENTON*) Oh. Oh, thank you very much.

*LUCY enters from the hall. She has obviously been crying and looks desperately worried. She is surprised to see KENTON.*

LUCY:          Why, hello, Inspector! Barbara …

*KENTON takes complete command of the situation, almost ushering BARBARA out into the hall.*

KENTON:        I must talk to you, Mrs Freeman. It's very important. Lady Barstow's just leaving.

BARBARA:       (*A shade embarrassed; indicating the bottle she is holding*) I came to borrow a bottle of sherry, Lucy. I hope you don't mind. The Inspector said …

KENTON:        (*Smiling, to LUCY*) I take full responsibility for the sherry, Mrs Freeman.

LUCY:          (*Puzzled, to BARBARA*) No … No, that's all right, Barbara.

BARBARA:       I'll phone you tomorrow morning.

LUCY:          (*Nodding*) Yes. Yes, do that …

*Still obviously curious and puzzled, BARBARA goes out into the hall.*

LUCY:          (*Tensely, to KENTON*) What is it? What's happened?

KENTON:        (*Standing in the doorway, looking out into the hall*) Wait a minute!

*KENTON stands in the doorway until he hears the front door open and close, and then he turns back into the room and faces LUCY.*

KENTON:        (*With obvious urgency*) Mrs Freeman, there are certain things I'd like to explain to you, but unfortunately … (*He glances at his watch*)

LUCY:          (*Puzzled*) Inspector, what is it?

KENTON:        Well … (*He glances towards the French windows, then turns to LUCY again*) Mrs Freeman, when your little girl disappeared, I thought we were up against a

194

conventional kidnapping case – a case which might ultimately develop into murder. Twenty-four hours after Janet disappeared, however, I received a phone call from a man called Wilde – Superintendent Wilde. Wilde's attached to the Special Branch. He told me that the kidnapping was merely a means to an end and that the people responsible were principally interested in your husband. You see, when your husband was at Prescott, he worked on a special moulding process known as …

LUCY: (*Interrupting him*) I know all that, Inspector. These people have been blackmailing my husband. They've even blackmailed him into leaving the country …

KENTON: We know all about these people, Mrs Freeman.

LUCY: (*Stunned*) What do you mean?

KENTON: (*Hesitating, looks at his watch again, doesn't quite know whether to take LUCY into his confidence or not: suddenly he makes up his mind*) We've had our eye on these people for some little time. We've known what's been going on, but we haven't been able to do anything about it. I know for instance that your husband wasn't responsible for the Calthorpe murder.

LUCY: But you brought that letter here. You deliberately …

KENTON:      The letter was a fake. (*Smiling*) I ask you, Mrs Freeman, would your husband have left it in the handbag if he'd committed the murder?

LUCY:        Who did murder Miss Calthorpe?

KENTON:      A man called Stevens. We picked him up about an hour or so ago. Miss Calthorpe was infatuated by him. Stevens was one of the people I've been telling you about. These people were quite determined to get a hold on your husband, quite apart from the kidnapping. It served our purpose to let them think they were succeeding.

LUCY:        Was Stevens mainly responsible or was there someone else behind all this – someone more important?

KENTON:      (Q*uietly, nodding*) There's someone else, Mrs Freeman.

*The curtains over the French windows are suddenly drawn apart and a plainclothes man – SERGEANT WILLIAMS – enters. KENTON turns towards him.*

WILLIAMS:    The party's arrived, sir!

KENTON:      (*Briskly*) Right! (*To LUCY*) Mrs Freeman, I want you to go upstairs and stay there until you hear from me …

LUCY:        (*Puzzled*) But why on earth should …

KENTON:      (*With authority*) Mrs Freeman, please! It's very important.

*LUCY looks at KENTON, then at the SERGEANT, hesitates, and goes out into the hall.*

KENTON:      (*To WILLIAMS*) You know what to do …

WILLIAMS:    Yes.

*KENTON crosses and goes out of the French windows. The SERGEANT straightens the curtains over the windows*

196

*and then turns and goes out into the hall. After a moment we hear the front doorbell ringing. The bell continues to ring for some little time. Finally, it stops ringing and we hear the opening of the front door followed by the sound of voices. After a moment, BARBARA BARSTOW appears in the doorway, followed by ANNA. She still carries the bottle.*

BARBARA: (*To ANNA, rather apologetically*) If you'd just tell Mrs Freeman I'd like a word with her, Anna. It won't take a minute.

ANNA: (*After a momentary hesitation*) Mrs Freeman's in bed, madam. I'm afraid I can't disturb her.

BARBARA: Oh … Oh, dear! (*She smiles at ANNA and holds up the bottle*) I made a mistake – or rather the Inspector did …

ANNA: (*Puzzled*) So?

BARBARA: It's port. I want sherry. I don't think Mrs Freeman will mind, do you, Anna?

*BARBARA crosses to the drinks table, looks at the bottles, then exchanges the one she is carrying for a bottle of sherry. She moves towards the doorway. As she reaches the entrance to the hall, LAURENCE HUDSON appears. He is carrying his hat and overcoat and appears quite pleased with himself.*

LAURENCE: (*To ANNA*) The front door was open, Anna.

ANNA: Yes. Lady Barstow's just leaving.

BARBARA: (*To LAURENCE, indicating the bottle she is carrying*) I borrowed a bottle of sherry and it turned out to be port.

LAURENCE: (*Smiling*) That's the sort of thing that happens these days. You can't be too careful who you borrow from, Lady Barstow.

197

*BARBARA is a little uncertain about this remark. She gives LAURENCE a look, then with a brief nod goes out into the hall, followed by ANNA. LAURENCE smiles and crosses down to the settee. He puts down his hat and coat and turns towards the door. After a moment ANNA reappears.*

LAURENCE: Tell Mrs Freeman I'd like to see her, will you, Anna?

ANNA: I think Mrs Freeman's in bed, sir – or having a bath, I'm not sure which.

LAURENCE: (*Pleasantly*) Shall we find out, Anna?

ANNA: (*Smiling*) Yes, sir. (*She disappears into the hall*)

*LAURENCE takes out his cigarette case, strolls round the room, stands for a moment looking at the picture on the wall. After a moment he turns and, picking up the lighter off the drinks table, lights his cigarette. ANNA returns.*

ANNA: I'm afraid Mrs Freeman's in the bath, sir. I told her you were here and she said could you wait?

LAURENCE: Yes, I'll wait. Thank you, Anna.

*ANNA goes out. LAURENCE stands for a moment looking towards the hall, then he turns and walks across to the drinks table. He stands by the table for a second or two, obviously giving some matter consideration, suddenly he reaches a decision and takes a small revolver out of his pocket and places it behind the bottles on the drinks table. Having done this, LAURENCE turns and goes over to the picture on the wall. He swings it away from the wall, extracts a bunch of keys from his pocket, inserts one of the keys in the lock and opens the safe. He takes out a bunch of documents, glances through them and then discovers the one he is looking for. It is the letter CLIVE received from JACK STAFFORD. LAURENCE returns the rest of the documents to the safe, locks it, replaces the keys, and moves the picture back into position. He stands reading the letter, occasionally consulting the extra typewritten pages of notes. He looks a shade puzzled. Suddenly he hears something and turns towards the French windows. Quickly, silently, he crosses the room towards the French windows and after a momentary hesitation, pulls the curtains to one side. JANET FREEMAN is standing in front of the French windows. LAURENCE moves back into the room, staring at JANET in astonishment.*

LAURENCE:   Janet! What are you doing here?

JANET:      (*Moving into the room*) Hello, Mr Hudson …

LAURENCE:   Janet – what happened? How did you manage to leave the house?

JANET:      (*Moving towards the door*) They came for me …

LAURENCE:   (*Quietly, moving towards JANET*) Who came for you, Janet?

*JANET moves towards the entrance to the hall. She has obviously been told to do this. LAURENCE slowly follows her.*

LAURENCE:   Janet! Did you hear what I said? Who came  for you? What's happened to Lynn – and the  others?

JANET:      The police took them away …

LAURENCE:   (*Still moving towards her, a shade tense*) When?

JANET:      Tonight …

LAURENCE:   (*Quietly, coaxing her*) Now, Janet, listen, dear … Did you tell them you'd seen me? Did you tell the police I came to the house one night and … (*He stops speaking, staring past JANET into the hall*)

199

*CLIVE appears in the open doorway, and JANET turns and runs towards him.*

CLIVE:          (*Quietly, to JANET, but with his eyes on LAURENCE*) Go upstairs, Janet, your mother's in the bedroom          …

*JANET runs out of the room into the hall. CLIVE slowly comes into the room, advancing towards LAURENCE.*

CLIVE:          You made a mistake, Laurence. (*Pointing to the  letter in his hand*) That letter was a bait – for your benefit. Miller never wrote it. Stafford didn't come from Prescott.

*LAURENCE looks at the letter, then after a moment he tears it up and drops the pieces onto the floor.*

LAURENCE:     (*Quite calmly, facing CLIVE*) how long have you known – about me?

CLIVE:          I saw Kenton this afternoon after they'd picked up Pelford.  He told me they'd had their eye on you for some time. He also told me what happened the night Nelson came here. The whole thing was a put-up job, wasn't it, Laurence?

LAURENCE:     (*Nodding*) Yes. I knew Nelson wasn't dead. It was a blank cartridge. We wanted to get you worried, Clive – so worried you'd be prepared to do almost anything.

CLIVE:          You certainly succeeded …

LAURENCE:     Later, Nelson got out of hand and we had to get rid of him …

CLIVE:          You mean, he'd served your purpose?

LAURENCE:     Nelson was a little too ambitious for my liking. Besides, he took too many risks. (*With the suggestion of a smile*) You can't afford to take risks in this business,

Clive. Expect the best and be prepared for the worst.

CLIVE: Are you prepared for the worst, Laurence?

*LAURENCE moves towards the room in the direction of the French windows.*

LAURENCE: I think so.

CLIVE: You've caused Lucy and me a great deal of unhappiness during the past few weeks. She even tried to commit suicide. Did you know that?

LAURENCE: Yes. (*Turning towards CLIVE*) But the child wasn't hurt. We didn't hurt the child …

CLIVE: I know.

LAURENCE: I'm sorry about Janet. It was Pelford's idea, anyway; although I don't expect you to believe that.

CLIVE: I don't.

LAURENCE: (*A shrug*) Very well.

CLIVE: Laurence, there's two things I don't understand. Two things I want to know …

LAURENCE: Well?

CLIVE: The night Miss Calthorpe came here – the night she picked up the puppet …

LAURENCE: Ruth Calthorpe came to see me. She had a message from Stevens. Stevens wanted me to know that Nelson had arrived from Paris and was staying at the Drake Hotel. That's why she mentioned the two names.

CLIVE: And Pelford? Why did Pelford telephone you and tell you about the exercise book? You must have known that …

LAURENCE: Pelford telephoned me because I asked him to. I wanted the girl on the

201

switchboard to hear the conversation. I knew she'd be questioned by the police. It was an excellent cover-up, Clive, so far as I was concerned. Besides, it enabled me to draw your attention to Pelford, which was exactly what we wanted.

*The curtains are drawn aside and KENTON enters the room from the French windows, followed by SERGEANT WILLIAMS.*

KENTON:     (*Moving   towards   LAURENCE*)   Mr Hudson …

LAURENCE:   Yes …

KENTON:     (*Briskly*) I want you to come down to the station with me, sir. I have a warrant for your arrest. It's my duty to warn you that anything you say …

LAURENCE:   (*Interrupting him*) All right, Inspector. All right, spare the details. If you want me to come down to the station with you, I'll come.

*The SERGEANT quickly crosses to LAURENCE and pats his pockets, feeling for any sign of a revolver.*

WILLIAMS:   (*Satisfied, nodding to KENTON*) It's all right, sir.

KENTON:     (*To LAURENCE*) This way, Mr Hudson.

LAURENCE:   If you don't mind, Inspector, I'll have a drink first.

KENTON:     I'm sorry, sir, there's no time for …

LAURENCE:   (*Interrupting him*) There's always time for a drink. I should have thought you'd have learnt by now, Inspector. (*To CLIVE*) Do you mind, Clive?

*CLIVE doesn't answer. He stands staring at LAURENCE. LAURENCE crosses to the drinks table. He stands for a moment with his back to KENTON. He appears to be mixing himself a drink and then suddenly he swings round facing KENTON and the SERGEANT. He is holding the revolver which he has picked up from the table.*

LAURENCE: (*To KENTON and the SERGEANT, tensely, with authority*) Now, do exactly what I tell you. Walk across to the window. Tell your people outside that I've left the house by the front entrance. As soon as I hear the car, I want …

*As LAURENCE speaks there is a sudden revolver shot and he falls forward, clutching his left arm. The SERGEANT immediately rushes to his side and takes possession of the revolver. LUCY is standing in the entrance from the hall. She is holding a revolver and looks dazed and a shade frightened. She lowers the revolver as KENTON and CLIVE rush to her side.*

CLIVE:      Lucy!

KENTON:    (*Taking the revolver out of LUCY's hand*) Mrs Freeman, you shouldn't have done that!

LUCY:      (*Desperately*) I heard him talking. I was so angry, Clive! I suddenly thought of Janet, and everything we've been through during the past … (*She is very near to tears*)

*CLIVE takes LUCY in his arms. KENTON turns and looks across at WILLIAMS who is holding on to LAURENCE. LAURENCE is obviously in pain and is clutching his left shoulder.*

WILLIAMS:  (*To KENTON*) I don't think it's serious, sir.

KENTON:    Take him out to the car.

*WILLIAMS nods and takes LAURENCE out through the French windows. CLIVE leads LUCY to the settee.*

*KENTON looks at them for a moment then follows the SERGEANT and LAURENCE out through the French windows. LUCY sits on the settee and buries her head in her hands. She is crying. CLIVE kneels down by the side of the settee and puts his arm on LUCY's shoulder.*

CLIVE:      Darling, don't … Please don't, Lucy!

LUCY:       (*After a moment*) I'll – I'll be all right. Get me a drink, darling.

*CLIVE slowly rises and crosses to the drinks table. He mixes LUCY a drink and then takes it to her at the settee. Outside in the garden there is the sound of voices and a car making a speedy departure.*

CLIVE:      (*To LUCY, holding up the glass*) Drink this, darling.

*LUCY looks up and after a momentary hesitation, takes the glass.*

LUCY:       What is it?

CLIVE:      (*Smiling*) It's whiskey …

LUCY:       I – I don't like whiskey. You know that, Clive.

CLIVE:      (*Smiling at her*) Drink it, Lucy.

*KENTON re-enters through the French windows. He is still carrying the revolver.*

KENTON:     (*To LUCY*) Are you feeling any better, Mrs Freeman?

LUCY:       Yes – yes, I'm all right now, Inspector.

CLIVE:      (*To KENTON*) What about …?

KENTON:     It's nothing. The bullet grazed his arm – he'll be all right by tomorrow morning. (*Holding out the revolver*) Is this yours, sir?

*CLIVE looks at LUCY.*

LUCY:       No, it's mine. I bought it a few days ago. My husband said he was going away, and I

204

|  |  |
|---|---|
| | thought if I was going to be on my own I ought to have … |
| CLIVE: | (*To KENTON*) I think you'd better take care of it, Inspector. |
| KENTON: | Yes, I think so, sir. (*He puts the revolver in his pocket: to CLIVE*) Are you going away, Mr Freeman? |
| CLIVE: | (*After a moment*) Yes, I am. |

*LUCY looks at CLIVE. KENTON looks at LUCY, then at CLIVE.*

|  |  |
|---|---|
| KENTON: | When? |
| CLIVE: | Tomorrow morning. (*Suddenly, smiling at LUCY and taking her arm*) We're all going away, Inspector – the entire family. I think we deserve a holiday, don't you? |
| KENTON: | I do indeed, sir. (*Pleasantly*) Goodnight. Goodbye, Mrs Freeman. |
| LUCY: | Goodnight, Inspector. |
| CLIVE: | Goodnight. |
| KENTON: | (*To LUCY, patting the revolver in his overcoat pocket*) And don't worry about this business – accidents happen in the best of families. (*He smiles and goes out*) |

*LUCY turns towards CLIVE and takes hold of his arm. They move towards the door and at that moment JANET appears into the doorway, having taken off her outdoor clothes, with ANNA close behind her. CLIVE and LUCY walk arm-in-arm towards JANET – who stands smiling at them from the doorway.*

# THE END

## Talking of Serials by Francis Durbridge

I am having a new study built at my home in Surrey, and a few days ago I stopped work on the film script I am writing and strolled across the lawns to see how the work was progressing. As I looked up at the new room, which is being built over my garage, my thoughts flickered back over the years to my first study, in my parents' home in the Midlands, and to writing my very first serial play *Send for Paul Temple*. That was in the autumn of 1937, exactly twenty years ago.

Since that day, apart from the Paul Temple adventures, I have written many serials – *The Broken Horseshoe, The Teckman Biography, Portrait of Alison, The Other Man,* etc – serials which have been televised, broadcast, 'novelised' and filmed – besides being translated into many languages. Indeed, judging by some of the letters I receive a great many people seem to be under the illusion that I invented the serial story! This is probably due to the fact that *The Broken Horseshoe* was the first television serial to make an immediate impact on viewers in this country.

But of course the serial has been with us for very many years and has taken many forms, ranging from the avidly awaited Dickens romances in *Household Words*, through the Pearl White silent-films, the excellent Edgar Wallace thrillers for which newspapers and magazines competed so eagerly, up to the fast-moving radio and television serials today.

Serials have changed a great deal, but I still think a primary essential of any serial is a strong story – which to my mind accounts for the success of many adaptations of classic novels. Without it failure is inevitable, and although a strong plot may be ruined by indifferent

207

treatment or inadequate casting I do not believe that any serial can survive a weak story.

Looking back at the first Paul Temple serials I find that they were much more violent and straightforward than they are today. Temple is still his urbane self but he tends to become involved in much more complicated mysteries and to encounter a rather more diverse and subtle set of protagonists.

Like most writers I am constantly asked how I think of the plots for my plays, and although there is no magic formula so far as I am concerned it frequently happens that the basic idea for the story develops from a comparatively trivial incident.

The idea for my new television serial occurred to me early this year when I was staying at a hotel in Baden-Baden. The first day I arrived I noticed two people – a man and his wife – sitting at a corner table in the lounge. They were Americans: a smart, friendly-looking couple; but it was painfully obvious that they were not very friendly disposed towards each other. For two whole days they quarrelled. Angry words shattered the peace of the lounge, the terrace, and even the garden.

On the third day I saw the wife at the reception desk surrounded by luggage and wearing a travelling suit and an expression of grim determination. The luggage was taken out to a waiting car, the wife collected her bits and pieces, and moved towards the swing-doors. At that moment the husband appeared from the lounge carrying what looked to me like a cablegram. He had obviously been searching for his wife, and in a matter of seconds he crossed the hall and presented it to her.

As she read the piece of paper an expression of utter bewilderment passed across her face. The next second she was crying bitterly and leaning on her husband's shoulder.

They left the hotel together about an hour later, and, curiously enough, seemed reasonably happy.

What has all this got to do with my new television serial? Well, *A Time of Day* is the story of a husband and wife who are on the verge of divorce and then suddenly find themselves involved in a larger and much more important problem.

## Press Pack

press cuttings about *A Time Of Day* …

### Two New Serials by Francis Durbridge

Tonight, that brilliant writer of detective novels and thrillers, Francis Durbridge achieves the rare distinction of having two serials beginning in the same week.

One of them, "*A Time of Day*," a six-part thriller starts at 8.30 on Television; the other, "*Paul Temple and the Spencer Affair*," an eight-part serial featuring the popular detective, Paul Temple, begins at 8 in the Light Programme.

In "*A Time of Day*," the suspense builds up, with Stephen Murray, as Clive Freeman, a research scientist mixed up in mysterious happenings. Raymond Huntley plays the detective inspector.

Who the real villain is, nobody knows, not even the cast! For the producer and the author are withholding the script of episode six until the last minute.

"*Paul Temple and the Spencer Affair*" should, like its predecessors, prove a gripping radio serial. Peter Coke plays Paul Temple, and Steve is played by Marjorie Westbury.

### They Don't Know

The cast of the new serial starting on Wednesday are making bets about which of them is the villain. Why? Because the story is by Francis Durbridge. The title is "*A Time of Day*."

Mr Durbridge has an odd technique which gets the best from actors. They never see the final script until after the penultimate episode has gone on air. That way they must play the part exactly as it is written. No actor can give accidental hints to the audience by tone of voice or his facial expressions. They are just as much in the dark as the viewers.

Even if the cast did know the ending in advance I am sure it would make little difference to the success of the story. Because Mr Durbridge is the most successful, and the best, of all who contribute mystery serials to television. He is also the creator of the famous Paul Temple.

**Western Independent**

### New Serial

Francis Durbridge who has a number of winners to his credit, has written a new serial "*A Time of Day*" which starts on BBC on Wednesday.

In a rather different vein from its predecessors, its central characters are a husband and wife on the verge of separating after emotional conflicts. Clive Freeman is a research scientist who has been working for the government in a secret but poorly paid job. His wife, Lucy, has persuaded him to go into business for himself. The business is a great success and he has prospered, but he is not happy.

At the opening of "*A Time of Day*" Clive and Lucy become involved with other mysterious characters, which take their minds off their immediate personal problems. The rest of the story you can see for yourself. It looks like being one of Durbridge's best.

**Birmingham Weekly Post**

### New Francis Durbridge Serial

Francis Durbridge serial fans will have to be quick with the switches of their radio and television sets this evening. Just as the new Paul Temple series, the first since April

1956, finishes on sound radio, a new mystery serial. *A Time of Day*, (8.30), starts on television.

*A Time of Day* is Francis Durbridge's seventh serial for BBC television. It is the story of a research scientist who has been working for the Government in a secret, but poorly paid job, and his wife, who persuades him to go into business.

The business prospers, but the scientist is not happy. His marriage is on the point of breaking up when he and his wife become involved in "mysterious matters."

Members of the cast, as well as viewers, are kept guessing until the sixth and last instalment on who is the villain of the piece. The final script will not be given to the players until after transmission of the fifth episode.

Stephen Murray, who was the doctor in a former Durbridge serial, *My Friend Charles*, is the scientist, and Dorothy Alison is his wife.

**Yorkshire Evening Press**

**Thirteen – and one of them is a villain!** by Clifford Davis

Francis Durbridge – who has been writing thrillers serials for twenty years – comes up tonight with "*A Time of Day*" (BBC 8.30).

Durbridge, who devised the Paul Temple series, has said that his new serial is moulded on different lines from the usual whodunnit …

Research scientist Clive Freeman (Stephen Murray) and his wife Lucy (Dorothy Alison) are contemplating divorce.

Clive, who has quit his Government post to start his own business, finds himself mixed up in intrigue, murder and a child's disappearance.

This brings Lucy and Clive closer to each other. Divorce is forgotten as the couple plunge "into unexpected adventures."

"*A Time of Day*" will be seen in six weekly episodes.

There are thirteen characters in tonight's opening instalment and one of them is the villain. But, to sustain the suspense, only the producer and Mr Durbridge know who this is.

No one else will know till they get the final script.

**Daily Mirror**

**Durbridge Strikes Again! b**y Gareth Bowen
Tonight (8.30pm) is born the first of many question marks … Francis Durbridge (creator of Paul Temple) has come forward with another mystery serial.

This one is entitled "*A Time of Day*" and it should be a worthy successor to Durbridge's past triumphs – "*The Broken Horseshoe*," "*The Teckman Biography*" and "*Portrait of Alison*."

This prolific storyteller disdains the usual technique of the serial merchants:

BIFF! … cracking introductions;

SLAM! … nerve-shattering "cliff-hangers" keeping one in suspense until the next episode;

YAWN! … acres of padding in between.

Durbridge has a mind like an elegant corkscrew; his plots keep us guessing from one minute to the next. Not only are we kept in the dark about his villains; no one is quite sure about the hero … or the heroine.

"*A Time of Day*" carries on Durbridge's pet theme, that of "ordinary" people caught up in events which mystify them as much as they do the viewers.

Tonight it's the turn of a research scientist and his wife about to divorce each other when they are suddenly faced

214

with a much bigger problem. Dorothy Alison and Stephen Murray play the puzzled ones; Raymond Huntley is a smooth detective-inspector.

**South West Echo and Evening Express**

**They're Gambling to Find The Villain…** by Kendall McDonald

The BBC does not encourage gambling. Let that be firmly stated before we begin – even if they do let the telephone microphones at racecourses eavesdrop on the starting prices.

But I have to report that tonight sweepstakes will start throughout the country on spotting the villain of the new Francis Durbridge television serial "*A Time of Day*" on the BBC Channel.

Not only that, but the cast themselves will run their own sweep for Durbridge and his favourite producer, Alan Bromly – this will be his fourth Durbridge thriller serial – never let the players know what will happen.

The script of the last episode – Number Six – is withheld from the actors until after transmission of Episode Five.

This, once again, let me hasten to add in view of the BBC's anti-gambling attitude is not because they do not want the sweeps to be "fixed" but because they believe it adds to the reality of the acting.

If an actor knows he is the villain, the temptation to let a sneer of sinister note into his voice must be well-night impossible.

Says Bromly, firmly refusing to discuss gambling: "Durbridge is noted for his clever plots and classic detection, but this time he has taken a more emotional line.

"In fact, for the first fifteen minutes you might think it was a husband-and-wife drama. This one is written on the

215

more emotional level, with not so many gimmicks or tricks like hypodermics. I think this is the best first episode he has ever written.

"He has delivered the goods again. He has had many imitators but personally I think he is the only one … His last episodes are usually as good as his first instalments."

**Evening News**

**A New TV Serial I Shall Not Miss** by Ivor Jay
I shall not miss "*A Time of Day*" on BBC television tonight. This new serial by Francis Durbridge has all the portents of being another holding and suave mystery. Remember how Durbridge's "*The Other Man*" riveted us to the carpet?

Tonight's cast are expert actors. In fact, for this kind of play I cannot think of a better team of players. They include Stephen Murray, Dorothy Alison (a brilliant, compelling actress) and Raymond Huntley.

As in previous serials by the same author, members of the cast, as well as viewers, are kept guessing until the last instalment on who is the villain of the piece.

The serial is in six episodes and the final one will not be given to the cast until after transmission of the fifth.

Surely Francis Durbridge – a native of Birmingham, by the way, today achieves a rare distinction. On the Light Programme I see there is another new serial by him. "*Paul Temple and the Spencer Affair*" making its debut at 8pm.

Offhand I can think of no other author to have a play on TV and one on radio opening on the same evening.

**Birmingham Evening Dispatch**

**Make A Date with This New Serial – It's Excellent**
I don't often recommend viewers to watch one channel in preference to another, believing that they will please

themselves, anyway. But it would be a pity if anyone missed the new Francis Durbridge serial simply for not knowing how excellent it promises to be. "*A Time of Day*" (BBC) started dramatically with the kidnapping of a schoolgirl just as her parents were on the point of getting a divorce.

We have as yet no clue – not surprising seeing as how there are five more instalments to come – as to who the kidnappers may be, apart from some mysterious references to a Mr Nelson, who turned out to be a puppet.

There wasn't a wasted moment last night and perhaps future instalments will clear up some points which at the moment are hard to understand.

Why should a police superintendent and an inspector pursue different lines of inquiry? Why did the solicitor and the parents not tell the police immediately they received a message and a clue? These may be minor details.

The atmosphere is tense, but Stephen Murray has always seemed to me to be over-taut. The cast, however, seems to have been chosen with great care – Mr Murray as the father, Dorothy Alison as the mother, Raymond Huntley as the inspector, John Sharplin as the solicitor (who seems so obvious a suspect that he will almost certainly prove to be above suspicion) and Annabel Maule as the teacher.

I strongly recommend the next five Wednesdays at 8.30pm as a date with the BBC.

**Bolton Evening News**

### Surprises Spring At Right Moment – New Durbridge Serial

A Francis Durbridge serial should serve the BBC well in those areas where it is competing with ITV. "*A Time of Day*" which started last night is one of those neatly tailored stories, full of surprises sprung at the right moment, which will make it certain that people will want to follow up the half-dozen mysteries that are indicated. There is really nothing new that can be devised in this type of serial play: the people and the setting are necessarily the comfortable middle class with cushiony homes and large cars into whose lives crime and bewilderment break with maximum effect, but the degree of skill can differ, and in the new Durbridge serial there is all the smooth efficiency of the master's hand.

**Manchester Guardian**

### New Serial Sets A Pace

Francis Durbridge, the Birmingham author, appears to have done it again, if one can judge from the first episode of a serial. "*A Time of Day*" on BBC television, started in low gear but whipped smartly into top.

Durbridge has the ability to drop a whole drifter-full of red herrings around without obnoxious scent.

It is an intriguing thought, if true, that the cast, all more-than-competent actors and actresses, do not know the end of the story.

The story, that of a little girl missing from her home is, unfortunately, only too topical, but I have no doubt that Mr Durbridge will give it a twist.

The only doubt I have is about a tv serial, any tv serial, which does not have episodes which are complete in themselves.

It may have been all very well to build and the tension and suspense and leave Pearl White hanging on the edge of a cliff until next week but these days people and busier, have more to think about. It is not easy to pick up the threads.

**Birmingham Mail**

**The Old Master Has Not Lost His Touch** by Philip Purser

Francis Durbridge celebrated 20 years in the cliff-hanger business last night with a new Paul Temple epic on radio and, thirty minutes later, a new BBC TV serial.

"*A Time of Day*" showed that the old master has lost none of his power of setting up a compulsive mystery in less time than it takes to blink.

The Freemans (top people, scientific sub-division), were on the verge of separation when their little daughter Janet disappeared on her way home from school.

Within a few minutes of Mr Durbridge's brisk story-telling the clues were piling up like autumn leaves: mysterious phone calls: a mysterious message: an exercise book suddenly found: a strange name casually cropping up which proved to belong to a sinister toy puppet.

It was all good stuff. Whether it all adds up when the time comes to reveal the plot remains to be seen. But, clearly, the BBC is taking its new Wednesday night serial seriously. It could be a distinct threat to ITV's Play of the Week.

**News Chronicle**

**Durbridge Is Gripping Any Day**

It was in 1937 that Francis Durbridge wrote his first gripping serial "*Send For Paul Temple.*" Now, exactly twenty years after, and following such successes as "*Portrait of Alison*" and "*The Other Man*," to mention but two, comes the latest piece of suspense, "*A Time of Day.*"

In some ways, of course, sound can only supply the highest tension, but for the next six weeks viewers can look forward with anticipation (and as the weeks pass a steadily increasing frustration) as this latest thriller from the Durbridge pen unfolds.

219

Judging from last night's episode the story appears to be a simple one of estranged husband and wife coming together over their kidnapped daughter. Do not be so easily deceived! Mr Durbridge has at least five more twists of the plot up his sleeve, and we can rely on Stephen Murray and Raymond Huntley to give us full value for money.

**Wolverhampton Express & Star**

**Durbridge Doubled** by Jean Blair

A combination of the old and new mediums and some slick dial changing last night brought us the first instalment of two new Francis Durbridge serials.

At 8 o'clock on the air there was "*Paul Temple and the Spencer Affair*," then a quick move over to TV at 8.30 for "*A Time of Day*."

It is, of course, too early to pass any real judgment on these as thrillers, but there is no doubt that the old master's hand still has its cunning.

In both, Durbridge got things moving quickly, and he contrived neat climaxes to bring us back next week.

And I don't think it should be difficult to keep the two quite separate in our minds, for Durbridge has been wise enough not to put Paul Temple on the screen.

We all have our own mental picture of that cool young man (though he can't be so young now), and no actor could ever bring him to life without annoying a great many of his fans.

**The Bulletin and Scots Pictorial**

**No Time Lost with Mr Durbridge** by Ramsden Greig

When a playwright wants to indicate that a character is struggling with a problem as often as not he sits him behind a desk and has him write furiously, then tearing up the sheets.

Rather in the manner of a television critic preparing a notice on a comedy show. That was how we found Clive Freeman last night in the opening scene of Francis Durbridge's new BBC serial, *A Time of Day*.

But Mr Freeman was not writing a TV notice. He was planning a divorce. One would think that that was enough trouble for any man at any one time.

Mr Durbridge, however, likes to lay it on thick, and within a matter of minutes had Clive Freeman's daughter kidnapped; had Mr Freeman tormented by mysterious phone calls; and, for good measure, had him batter down the door of his dressing-room to find his wife attempting suicide.

Until last night I would not have thought it possible that a man could have it so rough in the space of a half-hour episode.

Certainly no one is going to accuse Mr Durbridge of the common failing among mystery serial authors of marking time on Episode One while they introduce their characters.

Presumably the next five Wednesdays will be spent searching for the missing daughter. I for one will be following the search party now being led by Detective-Inspector Kenton. Mr Durbridge has whetted my appetite like a dry sherry.

The sound radio fan in our family suggested with a sneer that Mr Durbridge's celebrated sound radio sleuth Paul Temple could have cleared up the TV mystery in two instalments. Mr Temple is, however, otherwise engaged. The prolific Francis Durbridge has him at work on a new radio serial which also began last night.

**He Keeps Millions in Suspense** by Ross Percival

Never in all his twenty years of steering clean-cut heroes safely round dangerous corners has thriller writer Francis Durbridge had so much to show for his efforts as tonight. Look at this:

**8pm Light Programme**: Durbridge's newest radio serial – "*Paul Temple and the Spencer Affair*" – Episode 3.

**8.30pm BBC**: Durbridge's latest tv serial – "*A Time of Day*" – Episode 3.

**11pm Channel 9**: Durbridge's yesteryear film hit, "*Send for Paul Temple*."

Passing a hand over tired looking eyes, Francis Durbridge grins and says: "Ah, those commitments … there's an original film story to be written for a British studio. And there are books to do. And I have a contract to write one or two serials a year for BBC television on any subject I chose."

In Francis Durbridge you see proof that British viewers and radio listeners will maintain a man in considerable comfort if he has the know-how to whip up an acute sense of suspense.

Take him home in the Surrey town of Walton-on-Thames. It is large and valuable and called the Moat House. The garage contains a large grey Jaguar.

Take his London club. It is in Pall Mall, that large broad highway with the high social rating.

Take his holidays. They bite into six or seven weeks of each year, and generally find him out of England.

How lush it sounds … But do not confuse his life with the simple things like falling off a log.

Pen in hand he sits at his work with all the application of a meticulous bank manager.

He works long hours. And his life is geared to that workers' bogey – payments by results.

So far he has never lacked the pace and ingenuity to keep his public at a high pitch of curiosity. Nor a suitable cliff from which to leave his heroes suspended week by week.

"There's no contract with the BBC for the Paul Temple serials," he says. "I simply negotiate the sale when one is ready."

Temple has gone much farther afield than the Light Programme. He is known all over the English-speaking world – because of the BBC's transcription service – and in most European countries.

He is called Temple everywhere except in Holland. There they call him Paul Vlaanderen (Flanders). And instead of Steve, the Dutch prefer to call his wife Ina.

**The Man Who Makes Crime Pay** by Bryan Buckingham
Between eight and nine o'clock on Wednesday evening, the work of one author will attract a radio and television audience of at least 11,000,000 people. Impossible? Think again? The author is master of mystery, Francis Durbridge.

Every Wednesday for the past four weeks over 4,500,000 listeners have been tuning in to the Light at 8pm to hear *Paul Temple and the Spencer Affair*, the fifteenth serialised Temple adventure to be broadcast since Durbridge began writing them in 1938.

Half an hour later, at least 7,000,000 BBC viewers will have settled down in front of their sets to lap up 30 more minutes of Durbridge mystery, namely *A Time of Day* which began four weeks ago.

They say crime doesn't pay. Done the Durbridge way. It does.

He looks like any fairly successful businessman you'd encounter on a late morning train to Town. Medium height, 45, well-built, with thin dark hair, his only concession to flamboyance is a pink shirt under his expensively cut blue-grey suit.

A graduate of Birmingham University, he began writing seriously for radio in the early thirties when *Promotion*, a play he wrote about life in a department store, was received with acclaim.

"The man who encouraged me most in those days was Martyn C. Webster, who still produces the Paul Temple series," he said.

Since those days he has written millions of words about the adventures of Temple, which have appeared in books, strip cartoons, and films as well as on radio.

Since 1951 Durbridge has written seven serials for BBC television. Remember *The Teckman Biography, Portrait of Alison, The Other Man?*

"When a writer creates someone like Paul Temple," says Durbridge, "it sometimes happens that the character runs the life of the author. I decided that wouldn't happen to me. That's why I accepted when the BBC commissioned me to write television serials for them. It meant new characters, and a new medium."

**News of the World**

**Francis Durbridge Interview** by Kenneth Ullyatt
Down below the control gallery of Studio G, Lime Grove, Stephen Murray, Raymond Huntley and Dorothy Alison were pacing their mystery-clad way through the plot of the latest episode of *A Time of Day*, on a vain endeavour to track the crook who abducted little Janet Freeman.

It was the final run-through, just before zero-hour of transmission time for the weekly thriller – a zero-hour that thriller-author Francis Durbridge never misses.

"Thriller-serial writing is a specialist craft," says Durbridge, "and in a month or two I shall have been practicing it for twenty years. In fact, a lot of viewers think I invented the thriller story!"

*A Time of Day* has a curious impact on viewers, because this grim story of the abduction of a little girl, and its international sequel, is something that could happen to many thousands of families. Durbridge has that uncanny knack of hitting on perfectly ordinary, everyday situations which – even while you look at them – develop along sinister and interesting channels.

Hull born, 45 year-old Francis Durbridge might be a character stepping straight out of one of his own chiller-thrillers, for he is "ordinary" in that same fascinating way; clean-shaven, neat, precise, still a little trace of a Yorkshire accent, immaculately dressed, the City man perhaps … strong nature, Roman nose, firm cheekbones … and hard, penetrating eyes which seem all the time to hold you in a magnetic grip.

Durbridge has the Yorkshireman's dislike of time-wasting fripperies. He talks fast and all the time he talks, those eyes relentlessly survey the scene. Durbridge's eyes are his fortune; it is his shrewd survey of human nature, and of the little usually-noticed actions of men and women, that make his TV thrillers so *real*.

From a library above the garage in his spacious Surrey home, The Moat House, he produces a golden spate of Tv serials, novels, and film scenarios.

At the moment Durbridge is working about 25 hours a day and, although he refutes the suggestion, is coining a fortune. He has few rivals. His Paul Temple became one of the biggest money-spinners on radio, rivalled only by Dick Barton.

"I never wanted to do anything else but write," Durbridge told me. And after Bradford Grammar School, Wylde Green College and Birmingham University, he served his apprenticeship to the craft of writing by the miserable ordeal of writing dozens of short stories, only to have them rejected. By writing, revising and re-writing, he taught himself his trade.

"Luckily I did not waste too much time," he said, "for I began writing when I was still at school. It was about 1933 that I sent my first play to the BBC, Birmingham. It was a straightforward play, *Promotion*, about an adventure in a department store. Martyn Webster produced it. Then I did a sequel, *Dolmans*.

"Both these were written in my parents' study in their house in the Midlands, and as the broadcasts were quite well received, I was given encouragement to go on writing.

"It was not until the autumn of 1937, just over 20 years ago, that my very first serial play, *Send For Paul Temple,* was produced. I had always wanted to create a detective character, and, with Paul Temple, I was successful."

"How do you manage to make your thriller dialogue flow so successfully?" I asked. "Do you dictate each episode?"

"My writing method hasn't changed since the first story I wrote," he said. "I always write the first draft with pen. I can and do type but find the process of typing or dictating too disturbing for the first draft, so I use a pen. Then I retype it myself.

"This may sound a slow and rather cumbersome method but as few can read my writing except myself, it is really the only way! Next, I revise the typescript, and finally it goes to my secretary who produces not only the final clean copy but the 99 extra copies we need for filing and other purposes! The BBC duplicating department produce it in script form, of course."

"And is it really true that the cast of *A Time of Day* do not know the who-dun-it-line yet?"

"Yes, only the producer and I know the solution until the last week. It is not merely a mystery stunt. We feel that the actors will give a much more natural performance if the plot develops naturally for them – which of course it cannot do if they have the final TV episode at the back of their mind throughout the earlier episodes.

"I get a central idea and then I build up the theme, and rough out a synopsis of the serial. Alan Bromly (the producer) and I then discuss it."

Bromly has produced three of Durbridge's latest serials and they are an excellent team. Bromly uses "The Method" for making actors seem natural and quite relaxed. During rehearsals each episode is rehearsed normally. Then comes the moment when Bromly tells the whole cast to run through it again, using the exact lines of the script but *playing it in comedy!*

Then a second time it is run through with the instructions to get as much melodrama as possible. After these two deliberate distortions, the entire cast can get down to a properly-balanced delivery.

Durbridge, who has never attended first-day rehearsals, was ignorant of "The Method." Then he turned up unexpectedly, and stood open-mouthed in horror, hearing the cast turn his thriller-lines to broad comedy. Never has a writer heard his lines so properly murdered!

"Can you pass on the secret of thriller-writing to new writers?" I asked Durbridge.

"I don't know 'the secret.' I only know my method," he said. "Although I don't do so deliberately. I find that for television I do not create mysterious *people*, but usually manage to produce mysterious situations from the happenings of quite normal people.

227

"The railway detective in *The Teckman Biography*, the detective on the houseboat and in the school in *The Other Man* – and of course Det. Inspector Kenton (played by Raymond Huntley) in *A Time of Day* – they are perfectly ordinary detectives investigating the happenings of perfectly ordinary people."

Durbridge, ex-Birmingham University, believes in getting his facts correct for his TV serials. So he has became an expert criminologist. And unwittingly he exposed himself to the most flattering insult any TV author has ever received.

Duncan Lamont, the 'tec in both *The Other Man* and the film of *The Teckman Mystery*, had not met Durbridge when the latter serial was in rehearsal.

The dapper little man with the magnetic eyes was sitting in the corner of the studio when Lamont was relaxing and reading his script.

"How do you like it?" ventured Durbridge.

"Oh, its good stuff," said Lamont. "It sounds all so *authentic*. You know, this chap Durbridge must be a bit of a crook himself ....!"

"Ah, academically," said Durbridge, unsmiling. "Only academically" … and then went back to the studio above the garage to pen another serial, in a hand which only he can read.

**TV Mirror**

**Even Stephen Murray Guessed Wrong** by Elsie M. Smith

Six weeks of suspense ends tonight with the final episode of *A Time of Day* (BBC, 8.30). Viewers who watch the hard way – by trying to solve the mystery – will know how successful they have been.

They will be clever, however, if they have struck the right path among all the red herring trails that have been scattered over the past five episodes. Not even the principal actor in the cast, Stephen Murray, who plays Clive Freeman, guessed the ending correctly.

The cast, as is now well known, are kept as much in the dark about the ending as the viewers. They were not given their final scripts until after episode five last week.

"I was well out," Stephen Murray told me. "And so, I gather, was every other member of the cast. But we have all been so baffled we didn't even run a sweepstake on it this time."

Sweepstakes have been usual among the cast during the run of Durbridge serials.

All were sworn to secrecy about tonight's episode. Not even Murray's wife and daughter, who have not missed an instalment, have not been able to drag a clue out of him.

**Oxford Mail**

**On The Air** by Ivan Yates

The Francis Durbridge serial, *A Time of Day*, reached its exciting and finely produced climax last night, with the unmasking. This brilliantly professional thriller series on the BBC makes Douglas Fairbanks's playlets – four of which appear this week on ITV – look even more feeble.

**Durbridge Ties Up All The Ends**

In a packed half-hour last night thriller writer Francis Durbridge successfully tied up all the loose ends in his serial *A Time of Day*.

Author Durbridge roped in Scotland Yard's special branch, using short-wave radios, telephone tapping apparatus and a lorry full of police to help in the rounding up of the kidnap gang.

Clive was cleared of both the murders which at first had seemed his work, and little daughter Janet was returned safe and sound.

Lucy saved the day at the 11th hour by shooting the mastermind of the whole thing. But fortunately, she only nicked him, and Det.-Insp. Kenton turned a blind eye to her criminal action, thus enabling her to complete the fade-out shot of a happy family successful reunited.

It was a workmanlike, if conventional, piece of writing by Mr Durbridge, and producer Alan Bromly skilfully built up and maintained as much tension as was possible to squeeze out of the plot.

Of the cast I particularly liked John Sharplin, as Hudson, and Dorothy Alison, as Lucy.

**Brighton Evening Argus**

Printed in Great Britain
by Amazon